The Dead Swede

A Sheridan County Mystery

Erin Lark Maples

LODESTAR
LITERARY

To Terrilani, for the faith.

1

ELIZABETH BLAU TALKED AROUND the pencil between her teeth, as though it were a rose and her work a tango.

But instead of a paramour whirling her about a dance floor, she wrestled a canopy pop-up with Casey, her brother. Instead of feet stamping a rhythm across a Barcelona stage, he braced himself to boost her upward.

She set one foot in his palm and he lifted as she reached up to press on the crux of their tent poles.

"A little higher," she said, her voice muffled by the pencil.

She half-sat on Casey's right shoulder, one foot pressed into the platform of his hands. Her fingers negotiated a pin above her head that had failed to poke through the designated latch.

With a quick twist of opposing bars, the metal pieces clicked into place. "Got it!"

Casey released her foot, which he'd held while in a squat, and stepped back. She bounced on the balls of her feet when she landed, the memory of cheerleading years taking over.

"Tent, check." Elizabeth removed a twice-folded piece of yellow, lined paper from her back pocket. Pencil now in hand, she consulted the inscribed list and ticked a box with a flourish.

She ducked out from under the canopy to take in the full effect. With the frame in place, blue canvas stretched above, their booth had an official look.

Casey shook out his hands and cracked his knuckles. He brushed at the thighs of his jeans, then pressed on the small of his back. He rolled his neck side to side with a deliberate

motion. A cascade of small pops sounded in the crisp morning
air. "I need to get back on the mats. Getting older isn't for the
weak."

In his prime, Casey was a rodeo champ. He'd gone to college on a wrestling scholarship and picked up roping while in
Nebraska. He'd given up the arena lights for a booming goat
cheese business.

"I'd hardly call late thirties old. You aren't giving me much
hope," Elizabeth said. She reached for her abandoned breakfast burrito. The wrap rested in its crinkled aluminum foil.
She'd ordered her and Casey's meal from the cafe that morning. Lukewarm now, the combination of eggs and veggies was
still amazing. She took a big bite and chewed. Hot sauce
zinged against the roof of her mouth.

"Wait until you get there. Then we'll talk."

"Maybe if you hadn't followed the work hard, play hard
mentality to the letter, you wouldn't be such an old man."

Casey laughed. "Easy there. I didn't say I was ancient.
Creaky, but not decrepit. Not yet, anyway. How's the list
coming?"

"We've got the tent. Two chairs, the table, and the tablecloth. Oh, and this little tin of weighted clips Jo sent. I didn't
think we'd need them, but now that I've used some, I may need
to get a box of my own." Elizabeth set the list on the table.
With a twist of her wrists, she wrapped her hair into a bun
and jammed the pencil through its mass, anchoring the hair
in place. When a few strands threatened to escape, she added
a thermometer from the pile of brewing equipment strewn
across the tabletop.

Elizabeth had long hair—for the moment. Half wavy, half
straight, she'd grown it out for the ease of braiding and neck
warmth in the brutal winter. She told people she planned to
donate the length of it. The closer truth was that she wouldn't
fork out the money for regular trips to the salon. Couldn't
afford it.

Hair in place, list checked, Elizabeth gave a short nod of
satisfaction. *This day will go well.*

Casey reached down to pinch one of the weighted clips,
each in the shape of a plastic picnic basket. "Huh. Just when

you think you don't want to own any more stuff, here comes another invention."

"Pretty sure that's how we ended up with cars and fax machines—and look how far those got us."

"You got me. I definitely appreciate vaccinations and pour over coffee."

Liz scratched at her head with one hand. "Okay. Booth is set up. Tent seems secure. We've still got to claim our token bucket. How about you do that while I set up the coolers and the rest? The entry is under Blau."

"Can do. What about Leia?"

Leia, their newest family member, waited by the corner of their booth space. A big dog, the shade of a sandy beach, Leia attempted patience. Her body remained still, but her tail thumped the asphalt at the mention of her name.

They'd rescued Leia over the holidays. Over the months since, she'd become excited by the hustle and bustle up and down the street. A retired sled dog, she was athletic, eager, and energetic. Her head turned toward each new sound and smell.

"Better take her with you," Elizabeth said. She handed him the leash. "I'm not sure we can trust her around the bratwurst."

2

H ANDS ON HER HIPS, upper lip tucked behind the lower, Elizabeth huffed. The puff of air fluffed her bangs upward as she scrutinized their set up.

Elizabeth wound blue ribbons around the tent poles. She set a few sprays of hops at the front of their table. A friend from back home had overnighted the cuttings from her Seattle greenhouse. Elizabeth smoothed the tablecloth to flatten an imagined wrinkle and considered her tableau. About half the booths chose to decorate, but not all. She wanted Blau Brewing to stand out.

Casey returned with a bright orange, lidded plastic bucket with a slot cut into its top. Without ceremony, he plunked it on the tabletop. When he saw Elizabeth's brows draw together, he tucked the bucket behind the sprays of hop vines.

Casey shrugged. "So it's a little bright. This way, it's easy for people to vote. Besides, I kind of like the color. Persimmon is opposite the color wheel from royal blue," he said.

Aside from cheesemaking, Casey was a popular home designer. His clients were among the wealthy ranchers in the area. He'd graduated as a Cornhusker with a degree in architecture. People consulted him on everything from lap pool plans to their kitchen backsplash. "They're practically complementary colors."

Elizabeth shifted each jockey box an inch to the left, then angled them across the table. She added a vintage beer stein, a stack of business cards, and taped a sign to the front of the table. "That's it—I think."

"It looks great, Liz. Really good. People won't focus too much on looks, anyway. They want to try good beer."

"I care, Casey. I want it to be perfect. I want people to associate us with a whole new level, and not just the judges."

Casey flopped into one of their two folding chairs. He extended an idle hand to stroke Leia's flank. "I know today is huge for you, but it will be fine. I promise. You've brewed two phenomenal entries. You are practically unstoppable. Incredible brews. Not to mention, you've got a secret weapon." Casey waggled his eyebrows at Elizabeth.

"Your cheese?"

When he'd heard about the contest, Casey jumped at the chance to provide cheese pairings for her brews.

The business started as a hobby. A vegetarian, he had a half dozen goats whose milk he turned into cheese for himself and his neighbors. This evolved into a growing business with distribution into local specialty shops. First, he'd expanded into Montana. Next would be in Colorado.

"Well, yes. My cheese is fabulous, but I was talking about me as your hype-man."

"I'll take whatever help I can get. The competition could get fierce today. Meanwhile, do you think Mr. Hype Man could help me set up the food trays? Actual customers are on their way."

"Aye, aye, Captain." With an exaggerated salute, Casey reached for a third cooler under the table. He extracted some waxed paper-wrapped packages and set them on the table along with a jar of fig jam. Then he rummaged in the bag slung over the seat back for a pocket knife and portable cutting board.

Elizabeth was once again thankful for Jo's lists. Her best friend was a whiz at planning.

"Did you bring the apples? I want to slice them up to serve with the cheddar," Casey said. He unwrapped one of the packages. With the knife, he sliced careful rectangles of cheese. He then cut each slice at a diagonal to form triangles.

"We did. They were on the list."

The buzz of her phone against the tabletop interrupted Elizabeth's focus. She lifted the device to her ear, holding it in place with one shoulder as she slipped on a pair of food handler's gloves. While she spoke, she placed cheese slices atop crackers.

"How's my little buddy doing? Tell me all is fine, and you aren't calling from the hospital."

Jo's voice came through the speaker. "You go from zero to disaster quicker than anyone I know. Of course Rhett's fine or Clint himself would come to collect you."

Jo Wolf was the local sheriff's wife and Elizabeth's closest friend. She and her husband lived down the street from Casey's Cloud Nine Ranch. When Elizabeth was new, the Wolfs went out of their way to be like a second family to the Blaus. Sunday suppers became a weekly tradition. Jo was also Elizabeth's most dedicated babysitter.

"Sorry. I'm a bit on edge."

"We made the list together. You should have everything you need—right?"

"I know, I know, and it's a big help. These are good, old-fashioned nerves. Distract me with stories about my adorable child, please."

Elizabeth took a deep breath. Time with her son was precious. He was in the best of hands, but she still kicked herself for every minute away from him. Co-parenting with her ex-husband did this to her. Somehow, no matter how much time she spent with Rhett, it was never enough. While today could make or break her career, she was taking a day away from her son to shoot for her own dreams. Being a mother meant sacrifice. Anything else felt like guilty indulgence.

"So far this morning, we had pancakes and made birdseed pinecones. We managed to get most of the peanut butter on the feeders."

"Always a triumph." Elizabeth heard the sound of Jo's kitchen sink swish on. While she missed her son, she didn't envy the cleanup, post-crafts. "What's next?"

"Corbin asked if we'd stop by and check in on the kittens."

At the mention of the name of her crush, Elizabeth's cheeks flushed. Had there been a mirror on the exterior of the brick wall behind their booth, she knew how she would appear. "Oh?"

The sound of the sink hushed off. "He's trying to feed them as often as they are willing to eat, so I offered to swing by. Rhett will love it."

"That he will." Elizabeth's son adored animals of all sizes and shapes. A twinge of jealousy pinched tension into Elizabeth's spine.

"Don't be surprised if I sign you up for one—or six—of those tiny fur balls. Speaking of animals, have you seen the goats?"

"Goats?"

"Lulabelle, too." Shuffling sounds muffled the speaker. Elizabeth pictured Jo moving the phone from one ear to the other. "I'd heard Corbin brought a truck full of animals. A trailer, anyway. Got a permit and everything."

Elizabeth straightened a triangle of cheese atop a cracker. "To a brew fest?"

"Yep. Said people will get a kick out of them. Brought the friendly ones. Good advertising, too."

"Advertising?" Elizabeth was a parrot. She was reduced to repetition while the butterflies tumbled inside her stomach.

"For the goat business—remember? He and Casey planned it out. He's going to rent them out to trim down brush for folks. It's a revenue stream and keeps the goats busy. The trailer has a sign with his number. We'll see if anyone bites."

Corbin ran the most animal-diverse rescue organization in the state. He'd helped Elizabeth adopt Leia and helped Jo adopt her barn inhabitants as well.

"I see."

"You have fun today. Don't worry about us. We'll be drowning in cuteness for most of the morning. Get out there and win that thing.'

"Will do," Elizabeth said. Her tone betrayed the flicker of self-doubt she'd struggled to calm all morning. "Give Rhett a kiss for me."

"Count on it—and keep an eye out for Ryland. He's on his own over there today. It's his first big solo event."

When the phone went silent, Elizabeth shoved it into her pocket and looked around. People buzzed in and out of the tents on either side of theirs. Some wheeled shiny kegerators over to their own booths. Others set out custom glasses. Most went out of their way to shake hands with everyone who passed by their booth. These contestants operated like professionals. People prepared to win.

Elizabeth wished she'd added self-confidence to the packing list. Instead, she was a single mom who'd spent half her savings on new brewing equipment, a wing, and a prayer.

Come on, Liz. You've got this.

She turned back to her own booth, sparse but tidy. Casey worked on the placement of his creations to ensure an effective presentation. He'd topped each slice of manchego with a small dollop of fig jam. One tray complete, he moved on to slice the cheddar.

"Thank you," she said. Nervous energy flooded her bloodstream. Today had to go well. That was the only option. This was her ticket forward. There wasn't a Plan B on that checklist.

Casey looked up from his work. "For?"

"For not letting me face this crowd alone."

3

"LIZ, YOU'LL BE FINE. Better than fine. You'll be Leia when you buy her a new squeaky toy."

They'd learned that toys wouldn't last long in their house. Leia could take a toy from whole to squeaker-less in less than a minute. She eviscerated her toys with glee.

"She does have a pricey habit of destruction."

Casey slid the blade through the rich cheddar. He set the slice onto a stack in front of him and repeated the action. "You've made not one, but *two* flawless entries. Someone will notice you here, whether you take top prize or not. It's a small town. People who are looking for brewers like you."

Elizabeth rolled her shoulders back. *You've got this, Liz.*

She scanned the crowd. At the early hour, contestants and volunteers buzzed around the booths. Most were deep in preparation for the crowds to come. "Do you think anyone will have a name tag that says something like Hiring Manager? Because that would sure help me know who to make my new best friend."

"They'll introduce the judges at the opening ceremony. They'll have name tags, and you know one of them. Relax, it will be fine. It's not like their votes are the only ones that count. Everyone's opinion matters."

Elizabeth was now anything but relaxed. "Oh, good. If you need me, I'll be over here obsessing over everyone's opinion."

Casey unwrapped a second hunk of cheese and set it on the cutting board before he picked up the knife. The vintage, bone-handled blade made a clean wedge of cheese with each pass through the mass. "If you must panic, remember that judges count for more. It's weighted. Focus on them."

Elizabeth checked the tubing in the jockey box for the third time. "Stuff my panic down in my gut when the judges come by. Roger that."

Casey put a hand on top of hers in reassurance. "I know I'm biased, but you have one heck of a shot at sweeping the contest. Depends a bit on how many people show up. What beers they like. Either way, I've been attending this thing for the last four years, and it's a bunch of hobby brewers. Low pressure, I promise."

While this was Elizabeth's first Sheridan Tap Fest, she was no amateur brewer. She'd paid for most of her education degree working as an apprentice at a brewery in Seattle. She'd learned everything from infusion and decoction to the best hops for a lager. Elizabeth loved teaching chemistry, but she kept her brewery job, too.

Until she'd had her son and took six months off. The teaching job was still there but the brewery had replaced her. When she was married, she'd let Nick convince her to tuck her brewing equipment away to focus on being a mother. It wasn't until she'd had to sell her custom equipment to afford the move to Sheridan that she realized the extent of her loss.

Now, Elizabeth Blau was a single mom, determined to forge her own future. Show her son that she was capable, worthy. A person who could stand on her own two feet with pride.

She loved teaching, was thankful to have a job. But the pay wasn't enough to keep her solid on her feet, not with a son. Not with the hope of buying her own house one day. Casey was happy to have Elizabeth and Rhett as roommates as long as she needed. Elizabeth couldn't stay forever, though.

Winning this contest, earning the chance to sell her creations, was the next step in her plan for success.

"I appreciate the faith, brother. I wish I had it in myself."

"Me, too. I wish you could see how far you've come. See yourself through my eyes."

Elizabeth bit her lip and looked down at the sidewalk. She scuffed the edge of her boot against the rough surface, uncomfortable. Sometimes it was hard for her to hear kind words about herself. A rough divorce put her out of practice. She was still getting used to hearing them again.

"Hey! I saw that." Casey frowned at Leia as the dog licked at the tablecloth. He moved the cheese stacks to the center of the table. He lifted the cutting board and knife. "Now I've got to find someplace to wash these."

"I've got backups. Here." Elizabeth dug in a large reusable grocery bag. She'd packed the big tote with everything from tissues to snack bars. Preparation meant she could take care of any issues that may threaten her success. "Who won last year?"

"Tap Fest? Owner of a brewery here. Aged in whiskey barrels. Pretty tasty. The year before that was someone out of Big Horn. Super obnoxious guy. Wouldn't answer any questions. I'm not convinced he made that imperial stout on his own."

Elizabeth smirked. "Let me guess. You asked him out, and he said no."

"You know me too well. At this point, it's tradition for me at these things. Everyone's in such a good mood at Tap Fest. Maybe you can join me in the tradition."

"Getting shot down at a beer event? Traditions aren't always a good thing. Remember the tuna casserole?"

Casey groaned. Their mother had cut out a recipe from a Reader's Digest sometime in the eighties. She'd tortured the family with the meal at least once a month when they were kids. Tuna, Swiss, olives, and noodles, all baked into a gloppy mess. "She was always so proud that she'd made something from scratch. I didn't want to be one more thing that made her sad, so I ate that garbage. I can still taste the relish she used in place of greenery. Yuck."

"I'm all for new family traditions. Like winning this contest. My future—Rhett's future—depends on it."

4

HER BODY IMMOBILE, LEIA's eyes followed the feet of everyone who passed by their tent. Furry chin resting on two
front paws, she watched people scurry about. Some rolled
kegs, stacked boxes, and greeted each other. No one acknowl-
edged the pooch draped over the dog bed underneath the
Blaus' table.

"Do you think Leia needs a playdate?" The dog's eyebrows
lifted at the sound of her name.

Casey tilted his hands and paused his snack prep. "Like for
a tea party or something?"

Elizabeth squatted near the table and peeked under the
draped fabric at her pet. The animal gave a furtive wag of her
tail, and Elizabeth reached out to scratch under the dog's ears.

"I guess I was thinking she could use a dog friend. She went
from a large, loud pack to our rather small and quieter one. Is
that healthy?"

"Don't know. Is it healthy for people?"

Elizabeth thought about his question. She'd moved out to
almost the middle of nowhere to escape the size and pressure
of a big city. With more space came fewer people. She hadn't
stopped to consider if she missed the masses of people, the
intensity and noise of their lives.

Here, she had a small and tight circle. Her brother was her
rock, Jo was her closest friend, and there were a few others to
whom she was growing attached. *Is smaller better?*

Elizabeth's knees popped when she stood up from her
crouch. She winced at the sound. "Quality is going to trump

quantity in my book. The dating pool was bigger, but they weren't all solid candidates. I could always find friends who wanted to hit the town, but our conversations never went deep. There's nothing wrong with knowing lots of people. I think the key is whether you truly *know* anyone."

"Got it. Agreed. And putting 'Matchmaking for Leia' on the list Jo made for us."

Casey reached for the sheaf of paper. Elizabeth snatched it away. "I need to find a dog park or something. I know she loves us. I just worry we aren't enough for her."

"If there's one thing I've learned, it's that we can always find ways our life is lacking. The real strength is highlighting how it's awesome. I mean, look at her." Casey held his hands out toward the dog. "She's so awesome the mayor is petting her."

As soon as the words were out of his mouth, Casey did a double-take. Elizabeth followed his stare.

A man knelt in front of Leia, making kissing sounds and baby talk in their dog's general direction. "Who's a sweet little doggums? Yes, it's you. It's you!"

"Mayor Roberts," Casey said. "Good to see you."

The mayor wore a crisp pair of jeans, a button up shirt layered with a puffy vest, and a shiny new pair of boots. His hair waved against his scalp, a ski slope of black across his crown. Elizabeth swore he wore a little concealer under his eyes, powder on his brow. With one hand, he balanced a scooter, silver with light-up wheels. Elizabeth looked from the man to his transportation and back.

"Grandkids gave it to me. Said it would make me more popular with the younger voters," he said. He gestured to the handlebars. "Even gave me a bell for the sidewalks."

The mayor pressed a button on the side of a metal, puck-shaped object fixed to the handlebars. A chirpy jingle sounded in response.

Elizabeth raised her eyebrows. "Nice."

Mayor Roberts flashed her a smile. "No need to stop what you're doing on my account. I saw this gem of a pup and couldn't help but stop by and say hello. She is the sweetest."

"We like to think so," said Elizabeth. "You can give her a treat from the jar, if you want."

Mayor Roberts eyed the large, glass, lidded container that anchored one end of their tablecloth. The jar was filled with dozens of homemade peanut butter treats. Jo's contribution, she'd made them in case Leia wasn't the only four-legged visitor to the Tap Fest.

"Those look like cookies for people."

"Technically, you could eat one, but it'll be pretty bland. There's no sugar in the dog variety."

Roberts removed a cookie from the jar and held it out, flat on his palm. Leia accepted his offering. She crunched on the bone-shaped peanut butter biscuit while the mayor stroked her fur.

Elizabeth ventured a personal question of their elected official. "Do you have dogs?"

"Oh no. I'd kill to have one though. Maybe one day. I'd have to convince the missus." He brushed his hands together as if in signal of the change of topic and a wish to rid himself of cookie crumbs. "Well, I've got to get this contest rolling. I'm looking forward to tasting what y'all brought. Best of luck."

With a salute, the mayor balanced himself back on his scooter. He pushed off with one foot to wheel himself to the next tent. Elizabeth watched him greet the brewers with a handshake and a smile.

Casey stepped to Elizabeth's shoulder. "Judge number one. I wouldn't worry about him. He's the easygoing type. He'll spend the afternoon figuring out who the crowd wants to win. Then he'll vote to make them happy. Classic politician. He's more of a martini person, anyway."

"Got it. Is there a judge I do need to worry about?"

"If you want to win, absolutely. In fact, I'd watch your back."

5

E LIZABETH OPENED HER MOUTH to demand details. Before she could speak, blaring music drowned out all conversation along the block.

A red and yellow behemoth of a truck turned up Brundage and headed their direction. Bright striping lined its sides. A strand of plastic German flags fluttered against its length. Faux hops vines wound around the railings that ringed its roof. Four external speakers, one on each corner of the vehicle, blasted oompah music. The vehicle made a neat ninety-degree turn to park at the west end of the festivities, its full decor on display.

"It's a...fire truck?" Casey squinted at the vehicle, as if perspective could clarify his understanding.

"Pretty sure you shouldn't try to put out a fire with beer. Check out those taps."

Elizabeth pointed at the exterior of the vehicle. A slew of shiny handles winked in the sunlight. Each had a different design on the tap handle. Many were a traditional wedge of wood, smoothed and printed with logos. Others were intricate in their carvings. Maximum Brewing was painted above the row of handles.

The passenger door swung open to reveal a pair of legs that ended in red stiletto heels. A woman leaned out of the cab to assess her landing before choosing to disembark onto the asphalt.

She embodied the festival theme with gusto. She'd donned a beer maiden's dress, embroidered with a hops vine and topped with a crisp, white apron. Layers of petticoats lifted the skirt of the dress so high that it flounced with every step. When the woman landed on the sidewalk, she wobbled in finding her footing. Elizabeth pictured her as a sugar plum fairy, on her toes and twirling.

Two waist-length braids framed a round face, dimpled at the corners of her mouth. Eyes framed with long, false lashes blinked twice. Ruby-painted lips parted to emit a voice like tinkling glass. "Anyone order a Fräulein?"

Elizabeth groaned as the new arrival beamed at her captive audience.

Casey crossed his arms and nodded in the direction of the new arrival. "*That* is who you need to worry about."

"Is she some kind of über-German pro-brewer sent to crush us mere mortals with her detailed cosplay?"

"Worse. She's one of the judges."

6

"DEIRDRE SORENSON. SELF-PROCLAIMED SUPER taster. Grew up here. Used to work at the brewery. Last year, she packed up and moved to Fort Collins to work in the big leagues."

"Baseball?"

Deirdre reached back into the cab for her bag. She flipped her braids over her shoulders before turning to greet the crowd. "Guten tag, everyone." She waved with one hand, a flapping of her fingers.

Elizabeth hadn't noticed the driver because she'd been so distracted by the passenger. Now, she assumed the shorter man who emerged from the backside of the truck was the ersatz chauffeur. With mousy-brown hair and beat-up jeans, he faded into the background.

An older man separated from the crowd, ogling the spectacle that was Deirdre Sorenson. He slipped along the silvery side of the truck. Jaw clenched, he confronted the driver in a low tone. His bushy, white mustache held court over the heated conversation. The driver's face flushed crimson. After an earful, the driver stepped back and threw up his hands in frustration. Mustache guy shook his head and returned to the crowd.

"Brewing," Casey said. "She works for one of the corporate outfits. She's in the design process somewhere, for their smaller craft lines. Decided to come home for a visit. Grace us with her presence and wisdom, I expect."

Elizabeth watched the drama continuing to unfold behind the truck. After the older man's departure, the driver ran a hand over his shaved scalp. He landed a swift kick on the closed back door before he grabbed the handle to open it wide. He set a foot on the tailgate and pulled himself inside.

"All right," Casey said. "That's enough of a sideshow for me. Let's get ready to crush our competitors."

"Excuse me. May I have your attention, please."

A short, squat man struggled to adjust the microphone stand. His red Sheridan Tap Fest T-shirt had VOLUNTEER printed across the back. A second volunteer skipped steps on their way up to the stage to assist the first. The two consulted each other and then the device. They pressed buttons, unwrapped cords, and flicked the switch.

While she waited for further announcements, Elizabeth took in the scenery. Festival tents extended along the better part of a city block. People milled about every nook and cranny.

It had been a long winter, and folks were eager for a gathering. The spring breeze brushed their cheeks. While they'd celebrated the official seasonal shift, snow was still a recent memory. Elizabeth took hold of Leia's leash as the dog sniffed at the air.

A few familiar faces peppered the crowd gathered for Tap Fest. Elizabeth had begun to know the residents, learn their stories. Connie Ann had a floral shop and was allergic to mangos. Ed Hamatty had an insurance business above Bryce Taylor's wine shop. Together, the two had a coffee every morning and a cognac each evening. Their building was next to a western clothing store, outside of which there was a bench that was never empty. Two old-timers parked themselves out front rain or shine, saying hello to everyone who passed by. People were institutions in Sheridan, and Elizabeth was their apprentice.

Then Elizabeth's gaze met a pair of familiar dark eyes—Kade Michaels'. The man was hard to miss. Half a head taller than most of those around him, Kade did not fade into the crowd. Today he clustered with some of his employees from the garage. Raj, the mechanic who'd helped teach Leia a few tricks, tipped his chin in Elizabeth's direction. All wore Kade's Garage button-up shirts, effective advertising. She'd seen the logo in the Sheridan Tap Fest program under the sponsors banner.

A flutter kicked deep in her belly as Kade raised a hand in a brief wave. Elizabeth thought of the kiss they'd shared that past autumn. She tasted the plum wine they'd shared. The sour cherry of her lip balm, the bitter tang of coffee on his breath.

One sweet memory before Kade became an overnight father-figure to his nephew. Benny, Elizabeth's former student, needed intense support to work through his trauma. This took Kade's time and energy, and everyone was understanding. Kind.

For Elizabeth, the resulting distance had cooled their initial attraction to a simmer. She had no one to blame but the twists of fate that sent people on paths they didn't choose. As a single mom, she's felt the bone-crushing intensity of providing for a child on her own. She knew the weight of Kade's existence because she'd struggled under it herself. Was struggling now.

Kade equaled complications, a pressure bubbling below the surface. Elizabeth didn't want the flame to die out. She didn't want it to boil over and overwhelm them both, either. Sometimes, you had to set a wish down and walk away.

Elizabeth held up her hand to return a weak wave when a familiar voice startled her from behind.

"Liz, hey! Good to see you." Corbin Beck approached her with both arms held out for a hug. "It's been too long. How the heck are you?"

"Happy to see a friend," she said, and stepped into his embrace.

Elizabeth closed her eyes to savor the moment. His jacket smelled of straw and animals. The stubble across his jaw brushed her cheek, and she held on for an extra heartbeat. It had been too long, and she didn't want the hug to end.

She'd met Corbin when he helped her with Leia. Elizabeth had never had a dog before, let alone a unique breed with lots of energy. With Leia, Corbin helped Elizabeth build confidence in herself alongside pet care. He was the owner of

Burro Buddies, a rescue shelter that served a menagerie of animals. She'd gained a loyal, four-legged best friend along with a major crush on her coach in the process.

Recent new funding streams for his shelter meant Corbin had been busy over the winter. He'd built a new facility, moved the animals, and added a couple of staff members. Corbin had postponed Elizabeth's casual coffee invites. He said he needed to meet a contractor, pick up an animal, or take a business meeting. In texts, he'd explain and apologize each time. She ignored the sting of rejection but stopped asking him out. *I should wait for him to reschedule, shouldn't I?*

Over Corbin's shoulder Elizabeth met Kade's gaze again. The man frowned and pressed his lips together before he turned away from them. Elizabeth wanted to both insist it was only a hug and for there to be something worth Kade's scrutiny.

When they parted, Corbin flashed his irresistible grin at Leia. He stooped to stroke the dog and asked, "How's our four-legged friend?"

Elizabeth laughed. "You know, living a rough life."

Corbin laughed. "I can tell." He rubbed both sides of her big chest with his hands. "Who's our champion trainee?"

Leia thumped her tail on the ground, happy to receive the attention.

"I'm told you brought some goats. And Lulabelle."

Corbin stood up. His eyes lit up like a kid's at Christmas. "You haven't seen them yet?"

"Pretty sure I'd remember if I had."

"They're in the shade. Under the awning around the corner. Behind that black food truck." He pointed to the alleyway between the buildings. "I bet the smell is driving them a bit nuts. I'd better get them some snacks."

Elizabeth crossed her arms in mock surprise. "You of all people left a small herd of animals alone downtown?"

Corbin laughed. "They are tougher than a dozen humans put together. That said, I came early with a buddy to set up the corral. Make sure it's secure. We're keeping an eye on things."

Elizabeth thought of the goat she'd met in her single year of summer camp. It had followed her with its beady eyes. The animal stood atop a shelf while she and a friend mucked out stalls. Elizabeth was never sure if the goat was looking at her or through her, somehow.

Her only other experience with goats was Buck, Jo's rescue goat. Protective of his best friend Betsy, Jo's donkey, Buck was okay with people being nearby—until he wasn't. Once, the animal had stopped a brutal attack on Jo with one solid kick to a stall door. He was as tough as they came.

"Let me know when you want to see them. I'll take you. They've all got names. And you know Lulabelle. I've also got a box of ginger snaps in my truck, so they'll pretend to like us."

"I'd like that."

"When are you free?"

Before Elizabeth could reply, a screech erupted from the microphone.

7

"**G**OOD AFTERNOON. WELCOME TO the tenth annual Sheridan Tap Fest. I am so pleased to be here with you all today and to sample the excellent creations of our very own homebrewers. My grandfather used to say there wasn't any dispute that couldn't be settled over a few pints. Then he left it to my grandmother to brew them."

The audience chuckled. Mayor Roberts delivered his opening lines with the practice of a seasoned politician. Perfect timing and wrapped in a soft twang, he handed words out like candy, and the crowd ate them up.

"Like my family, the good people of Sheridan County know that life is about good company and a fine glass of beer. Today, we've gathered fifteen of the top home brewers from the area to compete. It's our job to find the best, and quite frankly"—Here, he leaned forward to whisper, drawing a circle in the air like a lasso—"*we* are the winners in this scenario."

The crowd cheered and whooped. People pumped their fists in the air. Others waved their hands in solidarity, their high-fives a rally for the cause.

Roberts beamed at their joy. A volunteer handed him a festival mug, and he lifted it high. The attendees matched his gesture, then toasted with their neighbors.

Each festival ticket netted the attendee one of the commemorative mugs. Emblazoned with the event logo, they held a dozen wooden chips. Ten plain tokens for tasting and two green chips for voting. The plastic vessels made a solid *thwack* when tapped.

"Proceeds from this year's tickets will be split between three of our local nonprofits. Your votes selected the food bank, the rotary, and our newest recipient, Burro Buddies."

A whoop let out from the crowd. Elizabeth looked to Corbin whose smile stretched from ear to ear. A few people nearby clapped him on the shoulder, and he nodded in gratitude.

"Now, your vote counts in the competition among the tents. Our grand prize is one-thousand dollars—to cover the cost of ingredients and a hunting tag or two." Roberts paused to allow more chuckles from the crowd. "And the winner will be a featured tap at Maximum Brewing. As our biggest sponsor, the brewery wants to celebrate the expertise of our home."

One of the people in the red volunteer shirts stepped forward to whisper in Roberts's ear. "I was just informed that not only will the beer be on tap at the brewery, but it will also be featured on their new mobile taphouse—during Rodeo Week!"

Roberts toasted the vehicle at the end of the block, and the crowd erupted into another round of applause. Many were fans of one of the oldest and most prestigious events in the state, the Sheridan WYO Rodeo. Others were happy the best beer would be available on tap. Most attendees were both.

This was the prize Elizabeth wanted, no, *needed* to win.

What had started as a part-time gig to pay her way through college became a hobby she adored, then a second job she'd loved. Teaching paid the basic bills, brewing paid for school loans and then some.

Her job at the elementary school was a joy, but it wasn't her passion. She missed teaching high school chemistry. The combination of chemicals, equipment, and math served as alchemy for her soul. Even the most reluctant student, chasing a lab credit, learned in her classroom. Until a spot at the high school opened up, she wanted to channel this energy back into brewing.

Selling her custom equipment to fund her move to Sheridan County had been tough. Over the last few months, Elizabeth had rebuilt her setup in Casey's barn, one bag of barley at a time.

Winning this contest meant a baby step toward a potential career shift. Opportunities. Last year, deep in the throes of a painful divorce, this had been a pipe dream. Today it was a true possibility.

Elizabeth did her work to be a viable contender. Casey and Jo were her flavor-profile experts as she tested and tasted recipes. A line on decent hops from her old brewing buddies back in Seattle and some local ingredients helped her brew two solid beers for the contest. She couldn't wait to get feedback from the crowd.

Roberts continued, "Once you've tasted your way through the entrees, place your green voting tokens in the buckets at your favorite booths. Your votes will make up half of the beer's final score."

Here, the volunteer who'd helped with the microphone mounted the stage. He lifted one of the promised buckets above his head. Rounded, like a bowling ball in glasses, the man was cheerful, energetic, like a Boston terrier. He beamed as he lifted the bucket, showing it to the crowd. Sweat beaded on his upper lip, and a sheen crossed his forehead. He brushed an errant lock of black hair off his brow. Wetness under his arms further indicated a busy morning of preparation.

"Thank you, James." With a nod from Roberts, the bespectacled man retreated into the masses. "Now, I realize that I am the only thing standing between you and the beer, so I'll get to the last of the official business. Judge's scores will count for the other fifty percent. At the end of the event, votes are tallied, and the winner will be announced. I want to introduce to you our judges for the event. First up is local barista, Gary Price."

Elizabeth startled as her friend took the stage, shaking hands with the mayor. She shouldn't have been surprised. As she was learning, there wasn't much Gary didn't do. A confirmed bachelor, he was a renaissance man.

Gary raised his own mug to the crowd. "Thank you, everyone. This is an honor."

James was back, and he handed Gary a small notepad and a golfer's pencil.

Gary manned the counter at Beans & Biscuits. A favorite stop for Elizabeth, the counter was the best place for a macchiato and the latest gossip. Gary had a knack for being a good listener and for wrangling the temperamental espresso machine into doing his bidding. A bartender at heart, many a customer left their troubles with Gary at the counter of Beans.

"Our next contestant hails from Colorado but is no stranger to Sheridan. Please welcome brewer Deirdre Sorenson to the stage."

A smattering of applause welcomed the woman who'd arrived in the rehabbed firetruck. Her petticoats rustled as she brushed past Elizabeth on her way to the stage. The scent of jasmine trailed her like a feathery scarf.

With short, quick steps up the flight of stairs, she joined the group at the microphone. In her spiked heels, she towered over Gary. He held his hands behind his back and avoided her gaze. Elizabeth was curious how well they knew each other.

"Thanks y'all," she said, flashing a row of pearly whites. Elizabeth spotted a gap between the lower front two teeth.

Mayor Roberts leaned toward the microphone to resume his spiel. Deirdre pressed forward, cutting him off.

"I know it's been almost a year since I've been gone, but I want to say how much I've missed you all," she said. "Through your support, I've taken my career to exciting places. I've made a real name for myself in the brewing industry. While I love Colorado, this place will always be home. I can't wait to taste what you have in store for me!"

Deirdre smiled in anticipation at the crowd. Some people clapped, polite, while others turned their eyes toward the booths, eager to start sampling.

From behind Elizabeth's shoulder came a gruff voice. "Give me a break."

Elizabeth looked over her shoulder. In her periphery, she saw the mustached man. His arms were crossed, lips pursed, eyebrows drawn together in disgust. As she turned back, she overheard a second grumble.

"She couldn't brew a good beer if the recipe was tattooed to her forehead."

8

E LIZABETH COULDN'T SHAKE THE venom in the man's voice.
Whomever Deirdre was to Sheridan County, she was
something very different to that man.

Elizabeth wove through the attendees and contestants
heading for the booths.

Casey met Elizabeth at their tent. "Where've you been? I
lost you in the crowd. I worried you got cold feet and took
off."

Elizabeth detached Leia's leash from the matching collar.
She looped the leash around a tent pole and secured it back
onto the collar. While Leia was unlikely to stray, Elizabeth
didn't want to violate any leash ordinances. Their dog turned
a reluctant circle and flopped on the provided dog bed.

"Cold feet? Never. My circulation functions at a steady
three feet per second, thank you very much. I saw Corbin,
that's all. Went to say hello."

"Ah." Casey raised an eyebrow as the corner of his mouth
tilted up.

Elizabeth frowned. "What is that supposed to mean?"

Casey busied himself with the jockey box lines, checking
their set up for the dozenth time. He'd crafted them from two
vintage Coleman coolers. Their emerald sides made the light
green hops pop with color. Casey knew how to make anything
look trendy and chic—even old camping gear. "Nothing. Or
rather, nothing if you tell me it's nothing."

"Casey, I—" she started. She wanted to tell Casey it was
nothing. Saying hello to a friend, that's all.

But it hadn't been. Not for Elizabeth. The months cooped up indoors while snow blanketed the prairie had given her time to think.

Divorce had been one of the most difficult events of her life. She couldn't stay with Nick, but leaving wasn't easy. Not with a son to share. She'd had to risk so much to couch surf with a brother she hadn't seen in a long time. Start over.

Elizabeth had met a great guy here, a neighbor of Casey's, but that ended in tragedy. She'd gotten to know Kade a bit, but that got complicated.

Fall down seven, stand up eight.

Corbin was easygoing. Kind, cute, a business owner. Easy to like. When she spent time with him, she pictured herself interested in someone again. Dating again.

"So I like him." *There, she'd said it.* "So, what?"

Casey bit back a full grin. He returned his attention to straightening the tablecloth. "So nothing. Just trying to be a supportive older brother, that's all."

Elizabeth returned Casey's smile. He meant it. When they'd reunited last fall, it had been awkward—at first. After the loss of Casey's best friend and former roping partner, they'd grown closer again. Casey wanted to make up for lost years when he could have been there for her. Leaving home at eighteen meant he'd missed many of the formative years in Elizabeth's life. Neither would allow that to happen again.

Crashing at Cloud Nine Ranch was supposed to be temporary. While she hadn't intended to spend more than a few weeks there, this had turned into a few months. They'd built a steady routine, now. One day, Elizabeth hoped to buy her own place, but for now, Casey's home was where she and Rhett needed to be.

"Right now, you can support me by passing out business cards. And don't you even think about playing matchmaker."

Casey drew his pointer finger in an X-shape across his chest. He stuffed a small porcelain stand with fresh cards printed with *Blau Brewing* in navy ink. The outline of a chartreuse hop icon with a double-B inside served as their logo. The cards were a last-minute vanity purchase. They gave Elizabeth a burst of confidence whenever she saw them.

"Why hello, you two. How are my favorite contestants holding up?"

Enid stood before their table, a tray of lidded coffee cups in her arms. Her mass of curly hair extended from behind a beaded headband like a mane. Wrapped in layers of amethyst and burgundy fabric, the owner of Beans was all vibrance and good cheer.

"Good. I think. Yeah, good. We've got two decent beers—"

"—two *great* beers."

"My brother is biased. But yeah, they are pretty great. Anyway, those plus Casey's cheese—"

"—and a lucky mascot."

As if on cue, Leia got to her feet, stretched, circled again, and resettled in the same spot.

"Yep," Elizabeth said. "And the wonder pup. I think we are as ready as we'll ever be."

Enid nodded. "Looks like it. I've got money on you winning. Gary is taking decent odds."

Elizabeth put her hands on her hips. "Wait a sec. Isn't a judge placing bets against the ethics of competition?"

"Oh, he's not betting. Just collecting."

"So he's the bookie," Casey said. "Totally innocent."

Elizabeth stuck a finger in each ear. "La-la-la. Say no more. I don't want to know."

"Don't worry. You're a shoo-in," Enid said. That pony keg of your coffee stout got me through a blizzard or two."

"I wouldn't have been able to make it without your roast."

Enid had offered the collaboration for Valentine's Day. They'd sold out of Dark Heart Brew in a week and had plans for future releases. Enid had kicked around the idea of adding a beer license to the coffee shop.

"Happy to claim a small part of your inevitable victory, then," Enid said. "Speaking of coffee, I'm passing out lattes to those who aren't drinking. Care for one?"

One of the strict Tap Fest rules was that contestants not imbibe. Elizabeth had to sign that she would abide by the rules. The ability to serve alcohol on a street in broad daylight came with restrictions.

"Thanks, Enid," Elizabeth said as she selected cups for herself and Casey. "This is an unexpected treat I didn't know I needed. How was your trip?"

During the slower months of late winter, the cafe owner liked to jet off to sunny beaches, leaving Gary in charge. Enid set her tray on top of a jockey box so she could pet the semi-sleeping dog. "Molokai was gorgeous, as always. Spent a night in Oahu, too. Eddie says hello."

Elizabeth blushed. Eddie was a sometime visitor to the area. A performer she'd met over the holidays, he was easy on the eyes and heaven to the ears. "How is he?"

"Fabulous, as always. Says he may actually be back one day. Has a few friends he'd miss if he was gone too long." Enid winked at Elizabeth. "Said he's always happy to host guests."

"Is everyone trying to set me up today?"

Casey smirked. "Hey, Enid, what's the story on Deirdre Sorenson? I kinda didn't think she'd show her face here again."

"You and me, both."

Elizabeth volleyed her attention between the faces of her brother and friend. "Someone is going to need to catch a relative outsider up on the gossip."

Casey bit his lower lip and glanced around them. He leaned closer to Elizabeth and lowered his voice. "There were some rumors last year. When she was a contestant."

"At Tap Fest?"

"She won, fair and square," Enid said.

"Maybe," Casey countered. "Fair, perhaps. But I'm not sure about the square."

"What happened?"

"Deirdre brewed a great beer. A märzen. Tasted like jasmine and citrus. I had some, and it was delicious. The crowd loved it. Everyone bought extra tokens for full pints."

Attendees could trade in five tokens for a pint instead of a taster. Many would sample until they found a favorite and then trade in for a full pint.

"Wish I'd had some." Elizabeth thought of märzens as liquid toast. "What was the problem?"

"The issue is that the first beer she produced in Fort Collins was a dead ringer for another contestant's entry."

"Not to mention her former employer's recipe book went missing," Enid said. "Including his recipe for a killer märzen."

"Yikes." Elizabeth knew the value of a brewer's notebook. Her own was a ratty spiral notebook she treated like gold. Brewers' recipes were more than lists of ingredients. They included timing, temperature, and other techniques that made for a unique beer. "And she just left town?"

"Pretty sure if she hadn't, someone would have chased her out."

9

E LIZABETH WANTED TIME TO mull over the gossip, but a line of thirsty people kept her hopping.

Each Blau sibling claimed a tap and a cheese tray. Elizabeth took over the Rosehip Sour with the manchego and fig pairing. Casey managed the Pine Tip IPA with the apple-cheddar stacks. Most attendees forked over two taster tokens, unable to resist.

Feedback rolled in. Most was positive, some perplexing.

"I don't drink pink beer," said one boulder of a man in a *Here for the Beer* shirt. He lifted the mug into the sunlight, his face pinched in scrutiny.

"It's more of an orangey tone," she replied. "From the rose-hips."

The man gave her a weary look. "All right." He tossed the taster down. "It's...nice," he said, then moved on to the next tent.

Guessing he won't be voting for Blau, she thought.

Mayor Roberts was an early visitor, tasting both brews but skipping the cheese. When he tasted the sour, he smacked his lips together. "Outstanding," he said, and winked at Elizabeth.

Elizabeth cocked an eyebrow at her brother. Casey shrugged.

For his part, Casey talked up the brewing process and cheesemaking with extra gusto. Elizabeth had coached him through the basics of brewing so he could give an overview of her process.

"We used Chinook hops. You can catch that on the back-side. Taste that hint of pine?" Casey was chatting with a woman a decade younger than himself. With a MISS WYOMING sash over her cowgirl combo of boots and jeans, she nodded as though she, too, were a brewer. She continued to press him with questions as his line backed up.

Her brother was an attractive man. Active and fit, he had a rugged look with a hint of mischievous fun in his smile. Still, she was barking up the wrong tree.

Honey, you're not his type, she wanted to say, but shrugged it off. Her brother was capable of peeling off the attention of a handful of admirers.

With these and other interactions, the first half hour flew by, and Casey asked for a bio break.

"Come back quick. Don't leave me stranded. Your fan club might be after me."

"Ow! Dang it."

The moment her brother took off, Elizabeth was over-whelmed.

When the festival opened, the sales booth was hopping from the start. Volunteers distributed mugs to the newcomers and sold extra tokens to those after a second round. Deputy Ryland meandered through the growing crowd, his lean frame a beacon in his tan uniform and hat.

Elizabeth struggled to keep up with demand. She jockeyed between the taps but tripped over a folding chair and bashed her knee into the table. She took a deep breath as she winced through the pain. A grimace tightened her face. She inhaled through her nose before returning to the customers.

Next in line was none other than Deirdre Sorenson.

"Hello there," the woman sang. Her voice verged on cartoon princess. Elizabeth looked for the flock of songbirds and Prince Charming on a trusty steed. "Are you all serving? I couldn't tell, seeing as you have a line of customers and don't seem to be handing out any beer. You wouldn't want to miss one of the judges, would you? Especially the only one with actual experience."

"My sincere apologies," Elizabeth said through her teeth. She thought about the teaching profession. Her coworkers complained about obnoxious parents more than they ever complained about children. If there was one thing she'd learned, it was how to survive conversations with insufferable adults. "I appreciate the presence and expertise of *all* the judges. What can I get you?"

"I'll take one of each," Deirdre said. "It's cute how you set out appetizers. Like a buffet or something. So...rustic."

Elizabeth fought the urge to glare. The woman made a show of sniffing the sour, swirling it in her glass, and taking a tentative sip. She tipped the rest down her throat. Behind her, those next in line watched the judge for assessment.

"You know," Elizabeth said, "beer doesn't oxidize in the glass like wine does. Swirling won't change the flavor."

Deirdre narrowed her eyes. "I know what I'm doing. This isn't my first rodeo."

Elizabeth willed herself to stay silent while she filled Deirdre's mug to the sample line with Blau IPA. "I'm not from here and all, but I never did understand that phrase. It's like you're expected to know everything by rodeo number two."

Deirdre picked up the mug and scowled over its brim. A man behind the judge snorted at Elizabeth's jab.

"Deirdre," Casey said, cutting the tension with his return. He lifted the apron neck loop over his head and tied the strings behind his back. His words rushed in alongside his body, an intentional push into the conversation. "Welcome home! Thank you for stopping by our little operation. Can I get you another taster?"

"I've had them both, thanks. I was getting to know your sister." Deirdre spat out the last word as though it was offensive to her tongue. "Great to see you, Casey. You've always been a charmer."

"It was a nice day for you to come north and visit all of us," Casey said.

"You should be thankful there's more than one face to your business," Deirdre said to Elizabeth. She flashed Casey a brief smile and flounced off into the crowd.

Casey turned to his sister and cocked an eyebrow. "What did you say to her?"

"Nothing. Well, mostly nothing. I simply shared a few facts and—"

Casey groaned. "She's not the type to be into your facts, Liz. If it isn't her idea, she doesn't want to know it."

"It's not my fault if she can't take a joke." Elizabeth filled another mug and traded it for a token from a woman with short, spiky purple hair.

"We can't afford to tick off any judges." Casey used tongs to place another apple-cheddar stack on a cocktail napkin. "She's one-third of the votes."

"Don't worry," Gary said, stepping up to the table. "This judge, at least, votes with his taste buds. Not his ambition. And don't mind Dee. She's like a Bichon Frisé. All bark and no bite."

"I hope you're right. Any bite from her would be venomous."

10

"HOW IS THE TRAFFIC over here at the Blau booth?" Gary tossed back his sample of the Pine Tip IPA. "You landed a great spot over here by the stage."

"Decent. We've yet to sit down."

A steady stream of people continued to present their tokens and mugs for samples. Several took notes, discussed the nuances of taste. Many tried to pay Casey for the snacks.

"Makes me think I should open a tapas bar," Casey said. He refilled one of the food trays. "Hey, sis, ever considered getting into wine?"

Elizabeth tilted her head. "I could make a run for viticulture. I'd have to source some serious grapes."

"Sign me up to be your first customer when you do," Gary said. He snagged another slice of cheddar. "It's only going to get busier today. Folks keep streaming in. They dug more mugs out of storage, some from last year."

Casey wiped his hands on a bar towel draped over one shoulder. "Any idea of the ticket sales?"

"Last I heard, several hundred. Biggest year yet."

"Good thing we have plenty of beer," Elizabeth said.

"But I'm going to need more apples. I need to get started on the next trays if we are going to keep up."

"I'll grab the extras out of the truck. I left them in the back seat. Maybe the extra cocktail napkins, too. Just in case." Elizabeth began to untie her apron strings.

"If you see any ice, we could use some more."

"We're out of ice?" Elizabeth eyed the jockey boxes that used ice to keep the lines cool.

"It's fine. We're at a beer fest. We are a bit low, but someone is bound to have extra."

Elizabeth shook her head. "I am not about to risk serving warm beer."

"They drink beer warm in Germany."

"This isn't your frat boy romp through Bavaria. Some beer is better warm than others, sure. Wine can be like that, too." Elizabeth thought of her conversation with Deirdre. The intensity and risk of competition. "But we need ice, Casey. I'll go get some."

"The ice is on me. I should have brought more. I'll go when you get back, run to the convenience store if I need to. Grab the apples. Check out the competition. The taps will last at least that long."

"If you're sure."

"Make sure to come back. I'll die if I get asked to explain your mash process one more time."

11

E LIZABETH DETACHED THE LEASH from its anchor and gave a short whistle through her teeth. "Come on, girl."

The dog stood, stretched, then gave a short shake of her head.

Casey tipped his head to one side. "When did you learn how to do that?"

"Lifeguard. Sixteen." Elizabeth smiled and took the keys from Casey. They were still learning about each other, the life they'd missed together.

Elizabeth struck out on the sidewalk, dog in tow. She would stretch her legs, grab supplies, and get her head back in the game. If she could get an idea of what the competition brought, what the residents liked, she could be strategic. Next time.

This year, she'd leveraged her brewing strengths. Next year, she would brew for the clientele.

Most breweries carried the standards: an IPA, a pilsner, a lager. A red or a brown, maybe a porter. Root beer for non-drinkers. In the summer, there would be a sour, fruit-forward, then a heavy stout or a barley wine in the winter. Maybe some experimentals. When the craft beer scene exploded a decade ago, there was a flurry of new breweries. Each tried to have its own gimmick. A few years in, and Elizabeth could predict what she'd see on the menu before she set foot in the door.

This contest was not only a relaunch of her skill set, it was a chance to stake her own claim on brewing. If her gamble paid off, becoming her own boss one day could become a real possibility. With a profitable side business, she could change the future for herself and Rhett. One keg at a time.

Elizabeth looped Leia's leash around her elbow as the crowd thickened. Leia was a big dog, easy to see. The problem came if an excited Leia wrapped a slack, nylon strap around another person—and took off. Elizabeth had learned that the hard way one day at the park.

Near the stage, a quartet of people in various states of decorative German attire squatted over long, zippered bags. Each had tiny felt hats that bobbed about as they readied for a performance.

One man removed a small wooden block from his bag's recesses and set it on the sidewalk. Next came an alpenhorn, a long, wooden instrument with delicate carvings at each end. Swirls and whorls decorated the spruce, along with several cloud formations. It was as though the breath expelled by the player was visible across the woodgrain.

"Boreas," the player said.

Elizabeth gave a slight shake of her head. "Hmm?" She hadn't realized she'd been staring.

The man pointed at one cloud with a face blowing air along the body of the instrument. "Boreas. A lesser of the Greek gods."

"Ah, yes. The god of the winter winds."

"Not the warmest guy in any sense of the word. But it was his brothers who caused more problems than they solved. For me, he has the endless power to move the air. I ask for his blessing whenever I play." The man put the mouthpiece to his lips and blew a few notes.

'Beautiful. How long have you been playing?"

"Forever," he said. "Seems like that, anyway. Since I was a kid. But there were a few years back there when I didn't play a single note."

"I can't imagine." She thought of the instrument, propped in the corner of a living room, its black bag collecting dust.

"Sometimes when things get hard, we talk ourselves out of our passions. Our own worst enemy and all that, you know?"

Elizabeth nodded. *Hadn't I been questioning my own ability to pull off a win?* "I'm looking forward to the concert."

"And the beer?"

"Not me. I'm a contestant."

"Ah. One of the all-powerful. A Dionysus. How goes the competition?"

Elizabeth bit her lip. "Between you and me? I'm a ball of nerves."

The man smiled. "Oh?"

"I've put all my savings and then some into my equipment. Winning would mean I can keep going. Turn a hobby into something bigger, sustainable. I'm busting my tail to provide for my son, give him a big life."

"What's so small about the life you have now?"

The question sank straight into Elizabeth's heart, as though he'd aimed with sickening accuracy. What gave a stranger the right to ask what ate at her core every day?

Instead of the face of a triumphant hunter, though, shining eyes and celebratory sneer, this man's expression was kind. Curious and patient. While the other players busied themselves in set up, he waited for her. Gave her space to think.

Elizabeth's defense mechanisms deflated, a soft whoosh between her lips. "Landing something at an actual brewery would be huge. It's one of those cycles where I can't land a job brewing until I make a name for myself, but I can't do that until I have street cred as a brewer. Make sense?"

He nodded and continued to wait.

"My life isn't small. Well, it is. In a way. I left everything behind to start from scratch. But now I can see my dreams, picture that big life—only I can't reach it. Everything takes so long to change. I worry I missed my chance to do something big. That by the time anything happens for me, my son will be out of the house, struggling in his own life because I took too long to get it together." Tears slipped down Elizabeth's cheeks. She clasped her hands together and looked down at them, avoiding the man's eyes. "I'm sorry. I'm rambling, and we just met. I didn't mean to lay everything on you like that."

"Don't ever apologize for having a strong drive. Or for wanting good things for your son."

Elizabeth brushed back a tear from the corner of one eye. "Thanks."

"I'll be sure to swing by your booth after we play. I'll need to rewet my whistle. I've got a vote to cast, after all."

"Blau Brewing," Elizabeth said, savoring the taste of the unofficial name for her business venture. It was short and sweet, like a delicate petit four.

"You've got this," he said. "One day, you will look back and see how far you have come. See how far today propelled you."

12

E LIZABETH LEFT THE MAN to his setup, stuffed her hands in her vest pockets, and continued the walk.

Booths stretched out from either side of the stage, like airplane wings. Flanking either end of the booths were half circles of food trucks. At the corner of Brundage and Main were pizza, crepes, Thai food—and of course, sausages.

Sixty pounds of muscle planted her paws on the sidewalk and lifted her nose to the bouquet. Elizabeth joined her, inhaling the promise of hearty fare. The spring breeze carried the aromas in waves to the pair, and each began to salivate.

"You know," she said to the pup, "the human ability to taste is about eighty-percent smell. I wonder if it's the same for dogs."

Leia cocked her head at Elizabeth, as if to question why they weren't gorging themselves that very moment. Elizabeth laughed and rubbed behind Leia's ears. "Come on. Truck first. Treat next." She gave a brief tug on the leash and put heel to pavement.

Elizabeth chewed on her musings about dog olfactory connections. *Do all animals have taste tied to smell?* She collected facts like seashells at the beach. This was a shiny conch, just past the surf.

Leia was reluctant to go. Her ears drooped, her pace slowed. Elizabeth watched the dog lament the growing distance between herself and the food. She perked up as they approached the west end of the festival. The cacophony of scent echoed the first.

Here was another set of offerings. A smaller, bright blue cart promised coffee and bubble tea. A large, black truck hauling a smoker offered barbecue. The beermobile held court at the center.

The duo would need to pass through throngs of people to get to Casey's truck. At each business, people waited in line. Mugs in hand, smiles on faces. Tap Fest had all appearances of a success.

Elizabeth's own car was a minuscule hatchback with a persistent rattling. It needed a date with the shop, but she hadn't had the nerve to risk a run-in with Kade. Kade's Garage was the best around, but Elizabeth was all chicken.

Casey had offered his rig for the day as it fit the jockey boxes, food coolers, kegs, dog, and two humans they needed to haul. A mammoth ranch machine, it was one of many that lined the streets.

Elizabeth spotted a gap between two of the food trucks. Enough space for a human to crab-walk through with an athletic dog and slide between the vehicles.

The truck generators hummed as Elizabeth sucked in her stomach. Leia followed behind. A few more feet and they'd be through.

"No. Absolutely not. He'll find out and then I'm toast." A low, angry voice was audible through the gap. Elizabeth froze.

A second voice, higher pitched, pleaded, "You know what this could mean for me. What it could mean for *us*. He barely even noticed last time."

"You weren't here to see what he did or didn't notice. Aren't things going well for you? Didn't you get what you wanted?"

"Come on." The second voice purred with new softness. "Pretty please? With sugar on top?"

"It's too big a risk. For me and for you."

Elizabeth held her breath. The cool sides of the metal trucks framed her face. Leia nosed the backside of her knee, as if to push her forward. A trickle of curiosity with a hint of danger tickled her spine, kept her rooted.

The first voice was a mystery. But the second, simpering voice belonged to Deirdre Sorenson.

The metal of the Smoked Oak's truck grill was cold against Elizabeth's thigh. She set one hand on the hood to steady herself and inched forward. The plastic of the truck's headlights reflected two shadowy figures beyond. From the sound of their voices, they couldn't be more than a half dozen feet from where Elizabeth and Leia hid.

"Don't give me that. This isn't for us. You never visit. You haven't found me a job. I'm owed more and you know it."

Lower voice, taller stature. Likely a man. But who?

"I had to get established," Deirdre whined. "It's different down there. This was my first chance to come up, and I did. Now I'm here. With you." Elizabeth heard the forced honey in Deirdre's voice as it dripped from her painted lips. Shadowy Deirdre reached forward to touch her companion.

"I'm not doing it." The shadow person appeared to cross his arms. "Find yourself a new golden goose. Some of us have to maintain a reputation here."

Deirdre stepped toward him again. Lifted a hand to his face. "Please?"

"I want to believe this is sincere. I do. But I can't protect you this time. If you get caught—"

"We won't get caught. How am I going to build a life for us down there without your support? I can't carry all of the burden."

The door of Smoked Oak opened, and the smell of smoked meat wafted in the air. Leia let out a whine and wagged her tail. Each *thwap* against the truck grill was like the strike of a marimba. Elizabeth swore under her breath and pushed out from her hiding spot.

Deirdre and the beermobile's driver stared at the intrusion. Deirdre dropped her hand from the man's face. The man frowned at Elizabeth. Deirdre glared at Elizabeth with an intensity that would melt a dish of ice cream.

"Oh, hello," Elizabeth said. "Just after some apples. Did you know there are more than seven thousand varieties of apples? Almost eight thousand at this point. They just invented a new one in my home state a few years ago. I'm from Washington. They called it the Cosmic Crisp. Come by our booth and try some."

Elizabeth's go-to social defense in awkward moments was to spill forth trivia. Like a waterfall after a snowmelt, this reflex was in full effect.

The man continued to watch Elizabeth as a bemused smile slid across his lips. Deirdre folded her arms and tapped her foot, irritation gaining momentum.

"Our booth is on the south side of the street. Blau Brewing. You can't miss us. We have dog treats. Organic ones. Homemade. I promised one to Leia here, so I'd better get going. Okay then. Bye!"

Before another torrent of facts could escape her lips, she made a beeline for Casey's truck, dragging Leia behind.

13

NAPKINS UNDER HER ARM and the promised bag of Cosmic Crisp apples in hand, Elizabeth navigated her way back to the trucks, Leia in tow.

The arguing couple was nowhere in sight. This time, the back of the beermobile rolled open. Its gaping maw led to a cramped storage area. A slew of kegs, a freezer, tap lines, and several coolers were crammed in every available space. Cold air from the confines brushed her exposed skin, and she shivered.

Elizabeth exhaled a sigh of relief when she and Leia squeezed back through the gap. She wove through the people in line at the barbecue truck on her way to the booth. After ducking around a couple comparing notes, she ran into the beermobile driver.

"Oof," she said, as the package of napkins fell to the ground.

The man scooped them up and handed them back. "Hello again, apple expert. By the way, I'll stop by on my break," he said. There was a small gap in his front teeth, a nick from a razor on the side of one cheek. He stood so close she could count the pores on his nose, smell the pine in his deodorant.

"Huh?" Elizabeth searched for the context for his comment from her panicked brain. Her mind kept spinning over the frustration she'd heard in his voice. His refusal to help Deirdre.

"Your booth. To try your beer. I've had a few brews in my day, and I know a good one when I taste it." He swept his arm toward the truck and winked. A silver band on his middle finger winked in the sun. "I'm sure I'll love what you've brought."

"Oh. Yes, of course. Great. Be sure to cleanse your palate first. The hypothalamus gets overwhelmed after too many flavors." Elizabeth clapped a hand over her mouth. Sometimes she was a flood of information.

"You're funny," he said. "I like that. And thanks for the tip. I'll be sure to make you my first stop." His grin spread from ear to ear.

Elizabeth pressed her lips into a tight smile. She willed a hole to appear in the asphalt and swallow her up.

This was the point in a conversation with a guy where it either got flirty or stayed focused. She would enforce the second while she plotted an escape. "How long have you been driving the...er...?"

"Beermobile? It's okay, I know that's what everyone calls it. She's a beaut, isn't she?" He didn't wait for her reply. "Boss gets all the latest toys. Custom-lasered taps, those fancy new plastic kegs. This is just his latest and greatest."

"It's certainly...impressive." The truck gleamed. Elizabeth guessed it had been washed and waxed. Prepared for the inaugural venture.

"We got it for a song. Boss wanted a better way to serve at weddings and bigger events, like this. Got last year's winner on tap, along with our usuals." He patted the side of the vehicle as though it were a prize pig.

"Who won?"

"Guy from deep in the mountains. He does all this cool lumberjack stuff. Gets beer from trees and fungus like syrup. Or something like that. Anyway, we carried his beer most of the last year. People couldn't get enough. He's back again."

Elizabeth wanted to hear more about what the owner liked. In her mind, she saw herself as this year's winner. Pictured the design on her tap handle. Smelled the heady scent of brewing on a large scale in a proper space. Wanted to prove herself a valuable resource. A potential employee.

"Your boss must have good business sense."

"Left me in charge. He wanted to be out in the crowd, shake hands, talk business. Can't tell him no." A scowl crossed the man's face, then lifted. "Besides, it's not like it's too much of a chore. I get to meet great people. Like you."

Uh oh. Get this back in line, Liz. "I know how that goes. Used to work in a brewery myself. Keeps you busy, but I loved it."

Elizabeth remembered the feel of the old mop in her hands. The surface was rough with age-created splinters. She would wind figure-eights across the sticky brewery floor. There were endless grain bags to move. Long shifts, cashing out tipsy customers who leered as they tried to give her their phone numbers.

There'd also been the ping pong tournaments. The regulars with fascinating stories of many lives lived. Experimenting with new ingredients. Perfecting the recipe of a crowd favorite.

"The price you pay for a shot at working your way up, am I right? I'm Tristan, by the way." He held out a hand.

Elizabeth shook it with her own. She and Tristan had more than their appreciation for beer in common.

"Elizabeth. I should get these apples back," she said. She'd been gone long enough and still needed to check out the competition. "And I owe my very patient dog a treat...or five. Nice to meet you."

Before she reached their booth, Elizabeth turned to look back at the beermobile. Tristan chatted with admirers of the mobile brewery, poured pints from the taps, a smile across his lips.

One new brewing contact made, dozens more waited for her in the tents.

14

T HE CLOSEST BOOTH BELONGED to a fireman.

He dropped that fact in every other sentence. If he hadn't, she could have guessed his occupation. Red coolers, chairs, and lights decorated the tent. He wore a red shirt that labeled him Chief of the Sheridan Fire Department. Leia growled at a life-sized stuffed Dalmatian. In a red plastic fireman's hat, the statue guarded the booth.

Two other firefighters joined their leader, a man and a woman. Between the three, Elizabeth couldn't tell whose biceps were bigger. Each had five playing cards on the table, one flipped upside down. Stud, Elizabeth noted.

The woman looked up from the table and smiled. "Hiya. Can we get you a sample?"

"It's hard to say no, but I can't," Elizabeth said. "Contestant here."

"Too bad." He tossed a couple chips on the table. "We firemen brew a serious red."

"I don't doubt it. Do you also own the beermobile?"

"Sheila? Naw, but she used to be ours, the best a firefighter could ask for. Sold her when we upgraded to a new engine. If she's not going to be saving lives fighting fires, this is the next best public service." The firemen laughed.

The woman flicked her eyes between the cards and her chip pile. Must have something good, Elizabeth thought. A flush or higher.

"Now we have Betty," the fireman said. "Come by and see her sometime."

"My son would love that."

Elizabeth wasn't sure Rhett would like the siren, the rush of the energy. Her son preferred the quiet company of animals. A fire engine may be too city for her precocious two-year-old. If she explained that firefighters rescued kittens from trees, he might be willing.

She wished the fire crew luck and moved on before Leia could set in on the Dalmatian. Elizabeth had seen what her dog could do with a small squeaker toy. She could only imagine the damage on a sizable, inanimate mascot.

The next booth belonged to a couple from Story. The tiny town had a single school with four classrooms. After closing the Banner school for the rest of the school year, Jo had made sure to find a job for Elizabeth. She'd become a jill-of-all-trades for the tiny Story School.

"You're the school librarian," Judy said. Brown curls streaked with silver framed a doughy face that smiled at Elizabeth. "The one who does the read-aloud for the littles. Our granddaughter loves those."

"That's me," Elizabeth said. She hadn't wanted to focus on her day job today. Once upon a time, she'd loved teaching. Now, reality was more complicated. Last fall, she'd been desperate, took the job available. This fall, she might have new choices. After the school year was up, she wondered if she'd return to teaching in the fall. "I didn't know you were brewers, too."

Otis and Judy Müller came from two strong German lines, Judy explained. She handed Elizabeth a thumbprint cookie. "A kulleraugen," Judy said.

"Our heritage is what makes our beer unique," Otis insisted. "Old family recipes, tried and tested for generations. We even import our barley."

Elizabeth palmed a handful of toasted barley from the dish they offered. She inhaled the earthy scent and then tipped the grains into her mouth. They tasted of sunbeams. Crunchy and sweet, one of her favorite snacks. "Heavenly."

"Our doppelbock will be tough to beat," Otis said. A mischievous smile played on his lips.

"Oh, stop," Judy said, giving her husband a playful push. "It's her first year, give her courage." To Elizabeth, she said, "He's teasing. Come and talk beer with us anytime. We're retired, so we have plenty of opportunities."

"Make it soon," Otis called. "We've been dying for a new brewing buddy.

15

M ORE BOOTHS OFFERED A porter that smelled of raspber-
ries, two other IPAs, and a radler. She devoured the
details of the brews and their makers. Strategizing.

Jo had urged Elizabeth to enter one Sunday over supper.
She'd paired a pint of Elizabeth's kolsch with Casey's fresh
mozzarella and declared it perfect.

Casey. Elizabeth checked her wristwatch. Fifteen minutes
too long. She thought of Casey, prostrate on the sidewalk as
thirsty people peppered him with technical brewing questions. Elizabeth walked faster.

The sight of the next brewer halted Elizabeth's advance.
Behind the table, tap in hand, was the man with the mustache
and a chip on his shoulder.

Instead of the deep brow creases of a frown, the man joked
with the people in line. He filled mugs as he talked, eyes
animated. In a shirt covered in palm fronds, tan pants, and
sandals, his scraggly hair gave him the appearance of Jimmy
Buffet.

"Hello there," he said, as Elizabeth stepped to the table.
"What can I get you? I've got a coconut porter and a su-
per-smooth pineapple lager."

"Unique. I like it," Elizabeth said. "Rain check? I'm a contestant. Elizabeth Blau, from Banner. Actually, I moved here
last fall. This is my first Tap Fest."

"Then welcome! I'm from somewhere else, myself. Call me
Buzz," he said, and reached out to shake hands. "Great to have
another brewer on the scene."

Buzz's skin was the shade of a copper penny, the backs of his hands and arms freckled like his cheeks. Tanning booth or spray-on, she guessed. His grip was warm and leathery, and she found herself liking her fellow transplant.

"Your beers make me want to take a vacation. Visit a friend." Elizabeth thought of Eddie Enos, the performer and descendant of rodeo champions. She'd met him that winter and couldn't forget his rich voice or their flirtatious banter. *You need to find a date, Liz. You're dreaming of men three thousand miles away.*

Buzz rested his knuckles on the tabletop and leaned toward Elizabeth. "Between you and me, I'm counting down the days until I can retire. Spend every sunrise at the beach. Been doing this a long time."

"How long?"

"Long enough to learn what's truly important in life," Buzz said. He knelt to give Leia a belly rub. The dog lolled on her side, tail thumping. "Like good companions and cold beer."

"I'd like to be you when I grow up," Elizabeth said. "Any advice for an amateur?"

Buzz rubbed at his chin, considering. Then he held a finger in the air. "Get to know what makes folks tick. If you ask them what flavors they like, most won't have a clue. Figure out what's behind their motivation to have a beer in the first place—that's where the money's at."

"Thanks," said Elizabeth. Her brows furrowed together in consideration. *Maybe Jo could help me make a list of everyone's motivations...*

"Easy there. Don't go too deep," Buzz said. He must have read her expression. "People will tell you in their own way, even if they don't have the words. Kind of like our friend here."

Leia watched Buzz, eager for another pat. Before Elizabeth could respond, Tristan bustled into the booth.

"Hey, Dad, I've got Carmen on the taps, Renee on the till. Okay with you if I head out and sample a few? I met a pretty—"

Tristan stopped when he saw Elizabeth.

Dad?

Buzz looked at Tristan, then Elizabeth, then back to his son. Elizabeth assumed she was the subject of an unfinished thought.

"Go ahead, but be back at two." Buzz clapped a hand to Tristan's shoulder, then pulled him close and lowered his own voice. "You know what to look out for."

"I'm on it," Tristan said. He gave Elizabeth a sheepish look and ducked out.

16

PINE BRANCHES AND AN axe wedged in a stump of spruce drew Elizabeth's attention. She should get back to the booth. Relieve Casey. But a line filled with the buzz of excited voices furthered her curiosity. *What does this person have that I don't?* Casey had said she should check out the competition. *What's one more booth?*

Boughs draped across the roof of the tent. Some extended over the sides, creating a canopy. The theme continued inside.

Instead of the typical folding chair, the brewer had a stump. Over the ringed surface, he'd draped a Buffalo Check blanket. The fabric matched his flannel shirt. He wore a woolen hat, sherpa-lined flaps over his ears.

The line for this beer stood twenty deep. Jockey boxes, made from camouflage coolers rested in a hollowed-out log. This sat atop a table draped in duck blind webbing. If ever a space represented woodsmen, this was it.

Elizabeth had to know what was on tap. What people were saying about it.

Leia pulled toward the Blau booth, but Elizabeth held her back. She tucked into the crowd, sipping their tasters. Others jostled past her to join the growing line.

"What are *you* doing here?"

Elizabeth didn't turn around. She knew that voice.

"Judging, of course," replied Deirdre Sorenson. "What they are paying me to do."

"You mean you swindled your way in," Buzz replied, his voice again inflamed rancor. "That dog has more qualifications to judge beer than you do."

"I can't believe you don't have any kind words for your former employee of the month." Deirdre smiled, slow and cat-like. "Oh well. This is one vote you won't be getting."

Deirdre pushed past Elizabeth, bumping her shoulder. She didn't turn around. Elizabeth could feel the wrath of Buzz's hatred from behind her.

"Come on, girl," Elizabeth said to Leia. "Let's get back before Casey sends out a search party."

"Gah!"

A force yanked Leia's leash, and the dog yelped. Elizabeth spun to find Deirdre tangled in the strap. She attempted to extract one high-heel and then the other from the entanglement.

Elizabeth held out an arm for Deirdre to grasp as the woman teetered on the pavement. "Are you okay?"

"Your stupid dog was in the way and I—"

Elizabeth shot Deirdre a warning glance. Leia chose that moment to backpedal on her feet for resolution. Deirdre gasped and clutched at Elizabeth's shoulder.

Deirdre said, "I'm sorry. I'm—not feeling my best. Can you please help me? If I go tush over teacup, this crowd will see everything. I've had enough humiliation for one day."

Elizabeth met Deirdre's pleading eyes with her own. She knew that look, knew the vulnerability behind the quaver in her voice.

"Hold on to me," Elizabeth said. She held a finger up to Leia. "Stay." The dog held her place as Elizabeth squatted to address the leash. Deirdre's hands pressed onto Elizabeth's back as she grabbed Leia's collar with one hand and unclipped the leash with the other. Like a snake, her hand wound between Deirdre's ankles, untangling. Trip hazard removed, Elizabeth clipped the leash back onto the collar and stood.

"Thank you," Deirdre said. Then she burst into tears.

"Look, Leia's fine. You're fine. It'll all be okay. Do you have any tissues?"

Deirdre swung her backpack under one arm and dug inside. "Sorry. I don't know what's come over me. No, that's a lie. I do know." She found a wadded tissue and pressed it to her face. "It's fine for a man to be ambitious. To want bigger and better things. To bend the rules to get what they want. But a woman?" Her voice was barbed with bitterness. "Hah. Right. You have to have every man's permission to want more, and they aren't giving it."

"I know what you mean," Elizabeth said. Deirdre's confession rang a bell of truth. Hadn't she experienced the same frustrations? "When I became a mother, it was like I was no longer allowed to want anything else. Having a child was supposed to be enough. There's no proof that ambition diminishes for fathers, so it's not like—"

Deirdre straightened her skirt and brushed at the folds. With a sharp intake of breath, she interrupted Elizabeth. "That's a sweet story. Maybe one day, you'll win this little festival. Get yourself a trophy." She plastered a smile across her lips. "Good luck."

17

"YOU KEEP SCOWLING THAT hard and your face will freeze that way. Or at least that's what Gram always said."

"I'm thinking."

"For someone surrounded by glorious beverages and without papers to grade, you aren't exactly bringing good cheer."

At the tiny school where she wore many hats, they had only a few students in each grade. She'd stayed up late to finish the last of the papers to leave her Saturday unburdened.

Her favorite essay was written by a timid fourth grader. He said he loved spring because he could return to riding his pony across the prairie grasses. Freedom, peaceful and serene. Elizabeth wanted to step into the scene he'd painted, relax a while. The brush with Deirdre left her shaken, spent.

The block continued to fill with attendees. Friendly greetings, dusty boots, and mugs of beer in every hand.

Back in the booth, Casey scooted over to let Elizabeth take over the taps.

"Do you know that judge?"

"Which one? I assume you aren't asking about Gary."

"Of course not. Deirdre."

"Not really. She's a townie, but I didn't grow up here. Justin never mentioned her or anything, if that's what you're asking. Why?"

Elizabeth had winced at the name of Casey's deceased best friend. She'd mourned him too, if in her own way. If Casey could say his name, she needed to practice the same.

"I guess I'm curious. It might sound silly, but it doesn't seem like anyone rolled out the welcome wagon."

"Could be a case of you seeing what you're looking for," Casey said. "Like that red car thing."

"Baader-Meinhof."

"Yeah, that. Got the apples?"

Elizabeth plunked the bag onto the table. Casey removed one of the beautiful red fruits and started slicing. She retrieved the half-moon pieces and stacked each atop a slice of cheddar.

"Go ahead and add some of the sage sprinkle," Casey said. "A pinch on top."

"Sage sprinkle?"

"I air fried some sage leaves, chopped them up. Mixed it with some Maldon salt. Gives it a little extra something."

"Did I miss the memo that we were actually entering a highbrow cocktail party? Since when do you make something called sage sprinkle?"

Elizabeth couldn't help but tease her brother. She'd missed out on too many years of opportunity.

"Taste one," he said. "Then see if you want to harass me."

Elizabeth put one of the appetizers in her mouth. The crunch and sweetness of the apple balanced the creamy tang of the cheddar. The salty, herbal mixture tied the two together.

As Elizabeth chewed the riot of flavor, she nodded at her brother. "When you're right, you're right, Casey Blau. This is one heavenly pairing."

"It's even better with the beer," Casey said. "Been thinking catering might be in our future."

"You might be onto something. That was one drop-dead scrumptious mouthful."

"Speaking of scrumptious, did you check out the brewer at that forested booth?"

18

"UNIQUE DECOR OVER THERE. I assume that's the guy doing the wild yeast brewing. Sounds cool, if crazy challenging."

Casey nodded. "Last year's winner. Rumor has it he introduced a barrel-aging process this year."

"Now you are torturing me with curiosity. I didn't stop by because you'd been here floundering on your own."

"Ain't that the truth. Someone asked me the length of our primary fermentation. I had to tell them you'd be back shortly for tech support as I am just the pretty face for the company."

"Ha. Ha."

"Now that you're back, I'm going to go for ice. I'll ask around first, see if anyone has a spare bag. If not, I'll drive to the convenience store. Should take me ten or fifteen minutes, tops. Unless I also stop by that booth..." Casey winked.

"Better hoof it. Your truck is blocked in. Getting out will involve inching out of a precarious spot or ramping up over the library lawn. I've read you only need an inch in front and an inch behind to get out, but not sure who can swing that."

"I want to meet that driver," Casey said. "They need to be teaching driver's ed."

With a wink, he left Elizabeth to step into her apron and snap on a pair of disposable gloves. Leah turned a neat circle and settled into the dog bed, her adventure paused.

Elizabeth poured samples for attendees while trading pleasantries and shop talk. The mood was cheerful, light-hearted.

At the stage, the alpenhorn players held court. Some attendees danced, many cheered, and ripples of mirth ran through the gathering.

Elizabeth thought of the street fairs and other public events in Seattle. The city would close down a block and fill it with tents. People would come and go, buy their vegetables, bouquets of flowers. They didn't stop to know their neighbors.

This event was different, though. The block became a reunion. A gathering for the town.

A breeze brushed Elizabeth's bangs off her forehead. She savored the moment with a deep breath in and out. This was her life. Her new life.

Casey burst her bubble of peace. He'd sidled up to her while she'd stood facing the music, eyes closed.

"Bad news or good news first?"

Elizabeth groaned. "Bad news."

"No ice in the booths. You'd think in a crowd this big, someone would've brought extra—"

"And that we would've brought enough to begin with." Elizabeth tried to bite back the sarcasm, but it was too late.

"Exactly. Ridiculous, the both of us. I'm going to ask at the trucks. Came back to get my keys, in case."

Elizabeth reached into her pocket for the braided lanyard that decorated Casey's key ring. "What's the good news?"

"I'll let you know when I get the ice."

19

ELIZABETH FROWNED AT CASEY'S retreating form. If they didn't have ice, the competition was over. Warm beer was for frat parties and camping, not competing against a lumberjack.

"Everything all right?"

Corbin stood before her, next in line.

Elizabeth pressed at her eyes with both hands. "Hi. Hello. I'm okay. Just...got lost for a minute. Would you like to try the IPA or the sour?"

Corbin held up one arm, a red attendee bracelet strapped across his tanned wrist. "Designated driver here. Nothing but root beer for me. They've got it on tap at the beermobile, and this puppy gets me free refills."

"Oh, shoot. Had I known, I would have brought some of Casey's soda. He made a chokecherry cola that's pretty tasty."

"That is absolutely what this festival is missing. I need to get in the ear of the planning committee for next year. Anyway, I just wanted to say hello. You looked a bit lonely in the big booth by yourself."

Over Corbin's shoulder, she could see Casey near the food trucks, returning with a plastic bag of ice cubes. *It's either now or risk an audience.*

Elizabeth started to ask if she could make Corbin dinner sometime, when a bloodcurdling scream pierced through the crowd.

Everyone within earshot turned toward the sound. Casey joined the throng of people who ran for the source of growing volume. Corbin sprinted close behind. The vacuum of tragedy pulled them to its source.

The stream of attention poured toward the portable toilets. They'd been tucked into the alley between the buildings at the western edge of the event. Close enough to be convenient, far enough to minimize offense.

Elizabeth grabbed Leia's leash. A jumble of voices and escalated shouts directed her forward. Leia attempted to sniff at the ground, but Elizabeth dragged her ahead.

They rounded the end of the booths and almost collided with Casey. He stood among those gathered, all staring at a spot in the alley. Panting from the jog, Elizabeth leaned forward to place her hands on her thighs to catch her breath.

As her lungs returned to equilibrium, the focal point swam before her. The cause of the commotion solidified, steadied.

Between the last two toilets rested a pile of tulle and ribbons, red and black.

Arms and legs, velvet and ribbons. Unmoving.

Elizabeth's mouth fell open.

Heels and braids. Silence.

20

ELIZABETH SLUMPED IN HER folding chair, numb. Casey paced behind her, crossing and uncrossing his arms.

"I feel sick," he said. "I need water. More air."

"Sit down," Elizabeth said. "You're making me nervous."

Casey hugged himself. "I saw a dead body, Liz. I am, as the kids say, *shook.*"

"What kids? When do you hang out with young people? I'm the teacher. Get a hold of yourself."

In the minutes after the discovery, the crowd hummed with energy, unsettled. People searched for jackets abandoned at the dozen round, white tables. Gulped the remainder of their drinks. Sent texts, looked around. Unmoored, they gathered in small clusters with neighbors, whispering about the find. A few continued to approach the booths, downing tasters as fast as they were poured.

Siren wails announced a pair of patrol cars. They screeched to a stop, an ambulance close behind. The driver angled the vehicle as close to the crowded alley as possible.

Saliva soured in Elizabeth's mouth as she watched a few people slink toward the exit. A bustle of activity drew her attention to the stage.

James was back. He wrestled with the microphone stand and flipped a switch. Mayor Roberts pushed around him to address the crowd.

"Folks. Given the...uh...recent events, we are going to need to cancel the festival."

Gasps and groans followed his announcement.

"What happened?"

"Who was it?"

"Guess we go home now."

Deputy Ryland commandeered the microphone from Roberts. "Please, everyone." The tall and lanky man dwarfed the city official. Ryland ducked his head to move his mouth closer to the microphone. "No one can leave. At least not just yet. We need you all to stay here for the present. Oh. I'm going to have to close all the taps for now. Thank you all." Ryland stepped off the stage to join two officers near the ambulance.

Murmurs and grumbles rippled through the crowd. Those in the vicinity of the stage wandered, uncomfortable and re-sistant, like penned cattle.

"This will go over like a lead balloon," Casey said.

The mayor regained control of the microphone. "I know we're all disappointed, folks. Let's agree to cooperate with our officials, so we can all go home as quickly as possible."

A roar of white noise filled Elizabeth's ears. She watched the liquid from a spilled beer leach out over the tabletop and drip onto the pavement, wasted.

21

A BLANKET OF QUIET fell over the festival. Attendees and competitors alike sought occupation, distraction. Each tried to ignore the activity near the ambulance yet couldn't take their eyes from it for long.

Two emergency personnel hovered around the area. Pictures snapped. Measurements taken. By the time they lifted the black, zippered bag onto the gurney, onlookers had shuffled away. They whispered in groups, shook their heads.

In the Blau booth, the siblings dealt with their own shock.

Elizabeth flitted from the taps to the trays. She checked the integrity of the tent poles and wiped down the tablecloth for the sixth time.

Casey stretched beeswax wrappers over each tray. He lingered over the corners, ensuring a seal. He leveled the stacks. Started another tray.

Elizabeth's patience waned. "Won't the slices turn brown?"

"The hefeweizen people gave me a lemon. I squeezed a wedge over them. Should be all right."

"Lemon and cheddar aren't a typical mix. High-acidity foods can curdle cheese."

"This cheese is solid, not liquid. I don't want to toss the food, so let me know if there's another brilliant option I'm missing." Casey slammed a crate on the tabletop and began to toss his tongs and other tools into it.

"Hey," Elizabeth said. She put a hand on her brother's to stop his motion. "I'm sorry. I can't think straight. I'm...upset.

Ticked. Furious. This was all such a waste." She waved her hand over their booth.

"Say what you want, sis, but this was hardly a waste. Disturbing and tragic at the end—but a waste, no. How many contacts did you make today?"

"A few. Not like major player contacts, but nice people. Home brewers."

"Exactly. We'll regroup, come back next year. Take the crown."

Elizabeth exhaled all the air in her lungs in one whoosh. She sucked in her upper lip and nodded. The edge of their tent roof flapped in the breeze as she joined her brother in collecting their detritus.

"Did you see anything?" Elizabeth asked some questions while her hands were busy. When eye contact wasn't necessary.

Casey's nimble fingers worked at the knots holding the hops garland to the poles on the tent. "What do you mean?"

"When you went to get the apples." She looked at him now, quizzical. "You were back there?"

Casey met her gaze. "I didn't see anything. Besides the after, that is."

Elizabeth slipped the tablecloth from underneath the jockey boxes. She lifted first one end and then the other to free the fabric. She folded it, corner to corner, until she could tuck its bulk under her arm. "All I can see in my head is the embroidery of her dress. I didn't even see her face. I'd talked to her. I keep thinking what a horrible place to die."

She stifled a sob and Casey gave her a hug.

"We need to get some space from here," Casey said, and patted her on the back. "They'll ask us some questions, and then we'll go. I'll make burgers. We can watch a kids' movie with Rhett."

"Portobello? With your gouda and arugula?"

"Is there any other kind?"

Elizabeth's smile dropped. "Where's Leia?"

22

ELIZABETH AND CASEY TORE from their booth.

"You head toward Main. I'll go west," she said. Casey was off and running before the words had left her mouth.

Elizabeth stopped at each booth between her own and the flashing lights at the end of the street. She looked around and below every table. Zipped between any possible dog-sized hiding place like a hummingbird after nectar.

Leia had only been with them a handful of months, but the dog had stolen their hearts. She became a member of the family, and Elizabeth's heart raced at her absence.

When she'd first found Leia, the dog was injured, alone, and all but frozen. Most would say that the Blaus rescued Leia, but Elizabeth knew it was the other way around. They would find her. There was no other option.

An officer blocked the way to the food trucks. Arms crossed in front of his broad chest, hat tipped over his eyes, and aviators masking his expression. The back of the beermobile yawned open, its taps still. Buzz would have Tristan cleaning up somewhere, busy and out of the way.

"Uh, hi," Elizabeth said. Sunglasses said nothing. "Have you seen a dog run through here?"

Sunglasses shook his head.

"Okay. Thanks for your help."

Elizabeth stood on tiptoes to look around the human blockade. Leia wasn't the type to run off, but on the Cloud Nine Ranch, she had room and permission to roam. The beige, sixty-pound dog was easy to spot against the snow-dotted prairie. Leia always returned to a whistle or a call.

Here, among the shades and sounds of a mourning, ambling crowd, finding her proved to be a challenge.

Sunbeams brushed Elizabeth's cheeks, soft and weak in the afternoon light. *Scan the booths,* she told herself. *Breathe.*

Each footfall had to bring her closer to discovery, so she pressed on. Raucous laughter burst out from a restless group of college-age guys. They circled a tall table, downing beers and cracking jokes.

A woman had died, Elizabeth's dog was missing, and they laughed without a care in the world.

One of the men pushed back from the table and bumped into Elizabeth.

"Watch where you're going!"

"Easy," he said, and raised his hands in the air. "No harm meant."

"Still. There are a lot of people here."

Another man in the group said, "Sorry for my idiot friend. We'll be more considerate." He had gray eyes, brown curls around his ears.

Elizabeth nodded, her anger abated. She returned to worry. "Have you seen a dog? About this high? Likely looking for snacks. Super sweet. Tan-ish, big ears. I can't find her."

"Haven't seen her," he said.

The first man looked her up and down, surveyed her like a piece of meat hanging in a butcher shop window. "Can I buy you a beer? Kevin here says we're going to be here a while. Might as well get friendly."

Elizabeth pushed past him and continued her search.

"Suit yourself," he called to her back. Laughter erupted from the group. No doubt Kevin was getting an earful about the cold shoulder she'd delivered.

Spruce perfumed the air as Elizabeth approached the forested booth. The line in front was at least ten deep. Attendees palmed handfuls of tokens. Most elected for a full pint given the circumstances. Above the booth hung a pine board. Spar Tree Brewing was burned into the wood. Fresh beads of sap seeped through its surface.

Familiar laughter drew her closer.

At the front of the line, Casey leaned on the table, one finger hooked into Leia's collar. He spoke with the man behind the taps. As the latter filled a mug for the next customer, Casey chattered away. When Leia saw Elizabeth, her tail thumped. Casey tightened his grip and followed the dog's attention.

"Liz. I found her!"

The butterflies settled in Elizabeth's stomach. Quieted when Leia nosed her hand, apologetic.

Elizabeth hugged the dog who licked her face. "Where was she?"

"Helping herself to my lunch," said the brewer behind the table.

For the first time, Elizabeth regarded the person manning the booth.

Gray satin lined the underside of the man's flat-topped, wide-brimmed hat. The hat came just short of brushing the top of the tent. The man must be six and a half feet tall. Maybe taller. Tweed vest, trimmed beard, and bright blue eyes were his only other adornments. This close, the booth swelled with the scent of trees.

"Leia!"

"She let me pet her afterward," the man said. "Almost a fair exchange for a bratwurst."

"Elizabeth Blau." She held out her hand which the man shook. His fingers dwarfed her own. "The thief is Leia, and it looks like you've met my brother Casey. Let me get you another sandwich."

"Daniel. My friends call me Danny. Thanks, but I'm not sure we're allowed to go anywhere at the moment." The man tipped his chin toward the emergency personnel in deep discussion.

"Rain check, then," Casey said. "I know my sister would love to hear about your brewing process. I help her, you know."

If hosing down my equipment in exchange for full kegerator access counts as help, she thought. Elizabeth turned to look at her brother. Twinkle in his eye, his cheeks flushed.

Oh.

"Sounds great," Danny said. "It's been so busy I haven't had much chance for conversation."

The line pressed forward. Two people joined for every one that left. "You're a popular guy. I'm sorry the contest is toast. From the looks of this line, you might be a worthy competitor."

The man pressed his lips together as he drew on the tap. "Me too. Though if Deirdre's looking down on us, she'd find it fitting she brought the party to a halt."

"You knew her?"

Danny nodded, the slow confirmation of regret. "She was my cousin."

23

E LIZABETH STUMBLED OVER HER words, unsure of the right response. "Oh...I...didn't...oh."

Casey whistled through his teeth. "So sorry. I don't know what to say. Were you all close?"

"Casey! You can't ask him that. He just lost—"

"She almost ruined my life. So, no. We weren't close."

The lights of the ambulance flashed across the Blaus' stunned faces as it inched away from Brundage, its contents still. The crowd gathered in witness, parted to let the vehicle go by, somberly silent at its retreat.

Deputy Ryland took to the stage, holding his hat against his chest until the vehicle was gone.

Ryland cleared his throat into the microphone. "Erm-ahem. Ladies and gentlemen. Please, listen up."

James scrambled to raise the stand to the speaker's height. He twisted each joint, finger-tight. When it was ready, he steadied the stand. Job complete, he stepped to the side and lowered his head.

"We appreciate your cooperation. The officers and I are going to need to begin taking statements, so we need your help a little longer. If we could have all brewers head to their tents. Guests, please take a seat at the tables. That will help speed up the process."

Complaints ran through the crowd. Elizabeth watched a few people press toward the deputy, lobbying their case.

Danny watched, silent. Elizabeth could only guess at the jumble of emotions in his mind.

Elizabeth said, "Casey, we'd better get back. Give Danny a chance to sort out his booth while we get ours packed up.

Danny touched the brim of his hat with one finger, a salute, and they left.

"You interrupted my game," Casey said. He'd given Danny a quick wave before they left.

"Game? You mean you drooling all over his product?"

Casey popped open one of the food containers and removed a cheese slice. "He brews beer in trees. Tell me how that isn't fascinating." Her brother stuffed his face with the snack.

"Wait. In...trees?"

"Now you're interested." Casey stacked the crate atop the coolers, folded his chair, and wrestled Leia's bed out from under the table. He tipped the mat against his pillar. "Lives in the mountains. Finds fallen conifers."

"And?"

"And that's as far as I got before you showed up and we learned he's now in mourning. Sort of."

"Forgive me for being focused on my son's best friend."

Bereft of her bed, Leia slumped over the lip of the sidewalk, head resting on her front paws.

Casey fished a pitcher out of his crate. He held it under the tap to drain the line. Elizabeth's hard work began to fill the container, soft bubbles rising to the surface.

"Oh no, the ice!"

Elizabeth remembered the bags. Long dropped on the sidewalk, what wasn't melted would be dirty. She lifted the lid of a cooler to assess. "It's almost gone. We have to keep these cold."

"Why is that? Aren't they sealed in the kegs?"

Ice crunched in the second cooler in response to Elizabeth shifting the keg inside. "If it isn't pasteurized, you've got to keep it cold. If we don't get some ice, we're done for." All their hard work, all the hours and every ingredient, wasted. There was a chance she could take her beers and shop them around. See if one of the two breweries in town would feature her. Give her a shot.

"I know, I know. Thirty-eight degrees." Casey shook his head. "I had the ice. I did."

"Maybe we can find some more."

Ryland approached their booth, deep in conversation with a Sheridan police officer. Elizabeth stepped off the sidewalk. If she could talk with him now, there was a chance they could get ice. Preserve the beer.

"If she had it, it's gone now," the deputy said. He kept walking.

The officer called after him. "That could be the motive."

Elizabeth gasped. *A motive?*

"People have killed for less."

She backed into the corner of their booth, hiding her face from the crowd. Her movement bumped the table. Jostled, the pitcher of beer tipped, then spilled. A puddle of her cherished sour gushed over the edge of the table and into the street.

"Liz!" Casey mopped at the table with a towel. "Don't spill it all."

Something was gone. Some*one* was gone. And according to Ryland, it wasn't an accident.

24

"LIZ. *LIZ.* E-LIZ-A-BETH."

"Hmmm?"

Casey scrutinized her. "What's gotten into you? You get excited over saving the beer and then you all but toss a pitcher into the street. I can't keep up."

Elizabeth watched as Ryland headed toward the volunteer tent at the corner of Main. She pressed the end of Leia's leash into Casey's hands. "I'll be right back," she mumbled. "Going to find ice."

Her brother's protests faded behind her as Elizabeth aimed for the front booth. Curious onlookers remained outside. The volunteers were idle without wristbands to pass out, directions to give. She watched as Ryland corralled James, the police officer, and another man off to the side.

Elizabeth slunk to the back of the booth. Cases of mugs were stacked at the corner. She had a veritable bird blind from behind which she could see and hear what happened inside the tent.

"Gone?" The mayor's voice pitched upward, betraying his surprise. "What do you mean, gone?"

Elizabeth could picture Ryland behind the stack of boxes. A thin mustache painting his upper lip. Boots in need of polish. Notepad out, ballpoint pen poised for documentation.

"They checked her bag. No pockets. That money is nowhere to be found."

There was a pause. Elizabeth pictured the mayor rubbing at his face with one hand, thinking. "How much?"

"All of it's missing," James said. "Stands to reason that all of it was taken."

"Walk me through everywhere the money was before it was gone." Ryland's voice had an edge of command. "Tell me who had access."

Later, her best friend Jo would ask how he did.

Jo counted down the days until her husband, a sheriff, could retire. Motivated was Jo's middle name when it came to cheering on Clint's likely replacement, Deputy Ryland.

"James took the cash out of the bank. We've got the receipt. After things got started, he handed Deirdre the envelope. When I read the winner's name, she would present the cash. We'd all shake hands and there's your Tap Fest. Should have been simple."

"Until she wound up dead," James said.

"Who'd she talk to?"

"She was a judge. Back in town after a year away. Must have talked to half of everyone here, if not more."

Elizabeth thought back to the kickoff. Deirdre on the stage, weaving through the crowd. Visiting booths and sampling beers. Thought of her arrival in the beermobile to a gawking crowd. Mayor Roberts had a point; Deirdre's role required contact. Lots of it.

"So she carries the money, talks to everyone, and when her body is found, the money is gone."

"Significant cash," said James. "Sounds like a motive to me."

"Not to me," Gary said from behind Elizabeth.

Elizabeth jumped, startled. He'd sidled up behind her, hands in pockets. She pressed a hand to her sternum and whispered, "Gary. Can't you let a girl eavesdrop in peace?"

"I could, but where's the fun in that?" With a wink, he ducked around the boxes and joined the discussion.

"Gary."

Elizabeth could see the trio nod in acknowledgement.

James said, "The cash was in a bank envelope. She arrived in that machine with Buzz's lackey, tracked me down, and demanded to keep the cash on her. Said she didn't trust me."

Ryland was quiet for a moment, then asked, "Did she show the money to either of you? Mention her distrust?"

"No," Gary said. His baritone was even. "Mayor Roberts and I were here early. Deirdre chose to arrive in style and all that. The first time we saw her was the same as everyone else."

Elizabeth fumed. Someone else had the money. *Her* prize money. She shifted from the ball of one foot to the other.

"That helps us narrow down the timing," Ryland said. "I'm going to need you to stick around for more questions. And James, we're going to need somewhere to interview folks."

"Deputy, are you looking for a suspect?"

"As of right now, I have to consider everything—and every-one."

Elizabeth mouthed the word. "Suspect?" She leaned toward the voices to ensure she heard his answer. Under her hands, one box tumbled forward, taking others with it. Plastic mugs spilled out of the fallen containers and clattered across the sidewalk.

Her hiding place revealed, the men gaped at Elizabeth. She plastered on her best approximation of an innocent grin before she stooped to collect escaped mugs.

"It's best not to stack boxes higher than one's head," she said, and deposited an armful of mugs into an open box. James scrambled behind her to pick up the rest.

"Ahem, uh, Ms. Blau? Could you please return to your tent? We'll be over to the booths soon."

25

CLOUDS PUFFED ACROSS THE sky, round and white. Like cotton balls rolling across a spotless countertop. Afternoon shadows snuck out from behind table legs, around cars, and out from under those who lounged for lack of better occupation.

From her post in the folding chair, Elizabeth watched a pair of pigeons trade places on the Lions Club rooftop. A man in a ten-gallon hat whistled "America the Beautiful" as he strolled past their booth. Leia snoozed.

Elizabeth slumped in the seat, legs extended ahead of her. Arms and ankles crossed, she extended one foot to stroke the flank of Leia's side. Casey had relented and repositioned the dog bed. Leia dreamed, one leg pawing the air.

Casey bounced a tennis ball against the sidewalk. A repetitive *thwop thwop thwop*, while he made phone call after phone call. First he'd called his distributors, then his accountant. Next came the shipper. His cheeses could now be shipped across the country.

Elizabeth listened to an extended conversation on the shades of purple tissue paper used to wrap each delicate cheese round.

"Go with the aubergine!" With that proclamation, she plopped back in the chair, sullen.

Leia looked up from her nap, concern in her cocked brow.

Casey covered the speaker of his phone with one hand. "Geez, Liz. All right already."

"You can only expect someone to listen to the nuances of stickers, recipe cards, and cellophane wrappers for so long."

With an eye roll, Casey returned to his conversation and closed out the call.

"The next time you are hoping for a change in conversation, you can ask, you know."

Elizabeth twisted against the chairback to face him and squinted one eye against an errant sunbeam. The afternoon sunlight sent its fingers between the buildings, touching everything it could on the way out.

"I'm going a bit stir crazy sitting here. If we can't win this thing, send us home already."

"Riiiight, and Ryland should let the murderer leave? The police will swing by later for tea, take a statement then."

Elizabeth threw a wadded-up paper napkin at her brother. "We don't know she was murdered."

Casey straddled his chair to face her, pressing his chest against his chair back. "Hang on a second. Ten minutes ago, you raced over here to tell me they're looking for a killer."

"Shhhh," she said. Elizabeth dropped her voice to a whisper. "Did it occur to you that if she was murdered, the killer could still be here? Among us. The last thing I want is for them to think I know who they are. Or for them to know that I think I know who they are, in case they aren't who I think they are and are someone else entirely."

Casey blinked at her. "Uh. Yeah. I didn't follow most of that but okay. No murder talk. Can we play cards or something, then? I don't know if I can take more of your rollercoaster of reasoning."

"Did someone say cards? Rumor is I'm quite the shark."

Elizabeth and Casey looked up toward the voice.

Danny Sorenson rose over the table. He glanced from them to the volunteer booth. "I snuck over here in the hopes I hadn't missed the charcuterie everyone is raving about. I'd love to taste them with the beer, but brewer's rules, as you know. Have you got any left?'

Casey's face lit up like a Christmas tree at the prospect of serving their guest. He rummaged first in one cooler, then the other. "Give me a sec. I can rustle something up."

Elizabeth handed her brother one of the napkins she'd tucked into the crate. Casey loaded it with cheese, the fruit, and with a flourish, the sage sprinkle.

Loaded with snacks, the napkin was a miniature feast. Casey slid it from his palm to the tabletop. "We've got my peppercorn and lavender goat cheese. There's also the plain variety with fig jam. Family recipe. Liz and I are trying to figure out what to brew next. Thought they might inspire us."

"Mmm," Danny said, around the first mouthful. He hadn't waited for Casey to finish his explanation before taking his first bite. "Sharp. Creamy. Intense but soft. Like a Guillermo Lorca painting."

Casey whispered from the corner of his mouth, "Is that a compliment?"

"Lorca is a Chilean painter who makes beautiful work...if a little dark. Unique stuff," Elizabeth said.

"Next time I harass you for trivia, remind me of this moment."

"Will do."

Louder, Casey said, "So, you like it?"

Danny nodded, enthusiastic. "You've got me wondering how my beers would pair. Maybe with a wild mushroom omelet. Some chanterelles, fresh eggs, a little butter. Heaven."

"Morels are more likely this time of year."

Danny scooted the napkin off the table and into his own hand, a new tray for Casey's offerings. "You're right. I've got a burn site or two I can check. Now that the competition is canceled, I'll have more time on my hands. Anyway, thanks." With a wave, Danny headed back to his own booth.

When Danny was out of earshot, Casey turned to his sister. "You have any idea who that is?"

"A really nice guy who brews what sounds like delicious beer?"

"He's the Dead Swede."

"Or rather, his great-great grandson." Casey straightened the table cloth, brushed at the fabric.

Elizabeth pressed both hands onto the table to steady herself. "Wait—the what?"

Casey waved his hand around at the tents. "The festival. It started in his honor. Named after an original brewer, his relative."

Elizabeth regarded the retreating form of Danny Sorenson. In her mind, she pictured him as an early settler. Add facial hair, homemade clothes, and a layer of trail dust. He had the look of someone who had seen history, taken note. "I can see it."

"Legacies mean something out here, Liz. People have staked claims on far less."

Elizabeth thought of the Hart Family. Remembered Justin defending his allegiance to the Ranch. Family drew lines where nothing else would.

"So, he comes from a long line of brewers. Even more of a reason to ask. He's cute, too." Elizabeth nudged Casey with her elbow. "Go for it."

Casey hung his head. "I can't do that. He's the kind you pick out silverware with. Get a dog—or two—and wear matching sweaters for Christmas pictures."

"Leia let me put her in a sweater for all of two minutes. Once."

Leia gave a plaintive moan. She'd sprawled on the concrete, awaiting change.

"Dog clothes are overrated. Enough about my love life. Here comes yours."

26

"OR RATHER, HIS GREAT-GREAT grandson." Casey straightened the table cloth, brushed at the fabric.

Elizabeth pressed both hands onto the table to steady herself. "Wait—the what?"

Casey waved his hand around at the tents. "The festival. It started in his honor. Named after an original brewer, his relative."

Elizabeth regarded the retreating form of Danny Sorenson. In her mind, she pictured him as an early settler. Add facial hair, homemade clothes, and a layer of trail dust. He had the look of someone who had seen history, taken note. "I can see it."

"Legacies mean something out here, Liz. People have staked claims on far less."

Elizabeth thought of the Hart Family. Remembered Justin defending his allegiance to the Ranch. Family drew lines where nothing else would.

"So, he comes from a long line of brewers. Even more of a reason to ask. He's cute, too." Elizabeth nudged Casey with her elbow. "Go for it."

Casey hung his head. "I can't do that. He's the kind you pick out silverware with. Get a dog—or two—and wear matching sweaters for Christmas pictures."

"Leia let me put her in a sweater for all of two minutes. Once."

Leia gave a plaintive moan. She'd sprawled on the concrete, awaiting change.

"Dog clothes are overrated. Enough about my love life. Here comes yours."

"I don't have a love life—" Elizabeth started to say as she followed her brother's line of sight with her own. Then she saw *him.* "Oh," she said, a soft whisper.

"Good luck," he said. "I'm going to find out if there are any toilets that aren't part of a crime scene."

Corbin crossed the distance from tables to booth as though he had nowhere to be and all day to get there. The easy stroll of a man used to calling his own shots. Cheeks aflame, Elizabeth took a deep breath and readied to greet her favorite dog rescuer.

Many applied that directive in a loose interpretation. Corbin was one of them. He'd spent the time visiting tables, booths. People standing in groups. Elizabeth watched him, the social butterfly, flit between those speaking in hushed tones. When you ran a business, relationships were essential.

Elizabeth had never been the one in charge, the one to give the orders. She'd worked for someone else since she assisted at a neighbor's lemonade stand at six years old. After four hours and having to pay a quarter for her own cup, she promised herself that the lemonade she squeezed out of life would be hers and hers alone. Elizabeth vowed to one day be her own boss.

Today was not that day. Corbin had his own animal rescue and dog training business. He had a five-year business plan, a groundbreaking facility, and growing notoriety. Elizabeth had a canceled contest and beer that was warming by the minute.

Elizabeth's shortcomings thrummed at the inside of her chest. The man on whom she was crushing made a beeline for her table. She fought the urge to tuck her hair behind her ear. To smooth flyaways brought on by stress and the breeze. *Just breathe, Liz.*

Corbin gave a half wave as he approached. "Not the beer fest I had in mind," he said.

"It's no Wiesn, that's for sure."

A half smile played across Corbin's face. "You've been to Munich?"

"No. I mean, I'd like to. One day. Millions of people attend that festival. Can you imagine how much beer I'd have to brew? I barely managed fifteen gallons."

Corbin laughed, his cheeks pink. "I have faith in your skills. You'd rise to that occasion, I have no doubt. Hey, I came over to talk with Casey. He around?"

The butterflies in Elizabeth's stomach dipped under the weight of disappointment. "He was just here. Can't be far."

"Good. I wanted to talk interiors. We've got the kennel sorted out, but my facility needs human quarters, too. I want to see if he's got room on his client list. If not, maybe he can recommend someone.

Elizabeth stood on tip toe to peer over the crowd. A scan of the street for the bright pop of his amethyst shirt pinpointed his location back at Spar Tree Brewing. "Over there. He's made a new friend. We both have." With her chin, she nudged in Casey's direction.

"I see. I'd go over there and interrupt, but..."

"He's working on his courage. Shouldn't be long now before he returns with either a date or to disappear under a rock."

Corbin nodded. "Been there. Would you mind asking him to call me? Looks like that will have to do for today."

"Of course," Elizabeth said. Before Corbin could move on to the next table, Elizabeth rushed through her plan before she could second guess herself. "Hey—Corbin?"

"Yeah?"

Elizabeth started at the cement, a tent pole, her hands pressed together in front of her body. Speaking could take courage. "Would you be willing to go out and get a bite to eat sometime? You know, together."

Corbin froze in place for a beat. It was as though his form became a department store mannequin. One arm forward, the other at his side, lips parted, knees bent.

Elizabeth had the urge to press a finger to his chest and see if he'd tip over backward. *Tush over teakettle*, as her grandmother used to say.

Corbin's silence lapsed. His smile took on a filtered sheen. "Uh, um. Wow. I'm really flattered. It's just that I'm seeing someone, Liz. An old friend. We've known each other forever but it wasn't until recently...anyway. You're great. You really are. I just—"

Elizabeth felt as though a brick had dropped in her stomach. Was dating humiliating no matter your age?

Corbin backed away from her booth, as though she were the lion and the table a cage.

"No worries. It's nothing. Just a friendly gesture." Elizabeth knew she didn't mean any of the last few sentences. They'd tasted false, bitter, the moment they'd dripped from her mouth. "Maybe we can get coffee sometime instead. Talk about business."

A screech from the microphone signaled the return of announcements. Elizabeth said a silent prayer for the transition. The faster she could sweep her ask behind them, the better.

"Everyone, everyone, please. We have an important announcement." Here, Ryland paused for stragglers to focus on him. "Everyone must move into the theater so we can continue our investigation. Please head for the doors, and the officers will guide you inside so we can begin questioning."

Elizabeth frowned. *Why keep everyone for questions? Unless everyone is now a suspect.*

27

S ILENCE PRECEDED CHAOS FOR exactly three beats.

For his part, Ryland conducted from the stage, both hands up, palms out, facing the angry people around him.

"Now, now," he said. "I will give everyone the same information once we are all inside the theater. Please head inside and take a seat."

"But all our stuff is out here!"

"Where do we sit?"

"What about the beer?"

Questions chased behind Ryland, like a comet's tail, as he parted the crowd on his way to the theater doors.

The WYO was an art deco masterpiece, built in 1923. Geometric shapes, a bold marquee, and glittering lights draped the building in a time warp. Unique to Main Street, it fit in as much as it stood out, a beacon.

A line meandered toward the front door. Reluctant, people relinquished freedom for the confines of the entertainment venue.

Elizabeth searched for her brother among the disgruntled. She'd had the foresight to snatch up Leia's water bowl but little else. The interaction with Corbin had left her mouth dry. In her mind, she replayed every interaction that suggested Corbin liked her. *She hadn't been completely off, had she? Why does it sometimes feel like people flip on a whim?*

She fought urges to hide behind pillars and duck out of sight from others on their way inside. The rejected. When they made it out of this, she owed Ryland a pecan pie for saving her from continuing humiliation. *When,* she reminded herself.

Around her, the pace was slow, but the conversational quips came like rapid fire.

"The humiliation of it. I hope that poor girl isn't watching from Heaven..."

"Tom said it had to be a murder. No one goes and dies in an alley by choice. You know, Tom has a nose for these things. What these police are thinking..."

"...couldn't the killer be long gone by now? I don't see why we have to suffer..."

Inside, the theater was stuffy. Everyone from the fest jockeyed for the least uncomfortable spot near the exit. Some spread out across several of the eggplant colored, upholstered theater chairs as though settling in for a long game. Others roamed the lobby, viewing the gallery of movie posters from prior screenings. Several made a beeline for the twin restrooms.

Elizabeth waited near the entrance for her brother. She'd selected a nook near a life-size cutout of Kevin Costner. This gave her the opportunity to duck behind should Corbin enter.

She could hear Jo now. "Are you planning to avoid that man for the rest of your life? Might make the dog training a little difficult."

That was the trouble with good friends. They always knew when to call you out. Jo was that person for Elizabeth. She knew which admonishments were coming.

People continued to stream through the doors. Many were wary, the excitement of the festival having worn off. The reality of the human corral, the potential hunt for a killer, sank in.

Students from Sheridan College had brought pretzel necklaces to the Tap Fest, a walking bar snack. Now, they crunched on the remaining pieces, necklace strings exposed. Elizabeth wondered how long they could go without calories. These students had the hungry look of athletes, possibly members of the rodeo team. Used to action, movement, a challenge. Sitting would not work for long.

The concession stand stood dark in the lobby. A rainbow of candy packages bricked the underside of a glass countertop. The popcorn maker waited, silent, alongside the soda machine.

If ever there was a need for food and beverages to pass the time, this was it. The docile crowd could turn unruly, deprived of their promised event.

Volume up in the theater itself, the line through the lobby slowed to a trickle. Elizabeth scooted out from behind Costner and peered through the main door. Main Street was quiet, unusual. A cruiser was parked at the corner of Brundage, lights still flashing.

Elizabeth wanted—no, needed—air, space, and a chance to regroup with her brother.

A group of lawmen were huddled in heated conversation outside. More likely to block her escape than not. She thought about using Leia as an excuse. Or a back door to the theater?

Then Elizabeth saw who had joined the conversation. She froze in place behind the propped open metal doors, unable to peel herself away.

28

A T THE DEPUTY'S SIDE were Gary and Buzz. Each man was the picture of discomfort.

Gary couldn't stand still. He looked to the left, then the right, and then at the ground. He rubbed the back of his head with one hand. Sweat stains darkened the underarms of his shirt despite the mild day. From what Elizabeth knew of the judge, Gary could not stand a wardrobe malfunction. He was fastidious at work, switching out his apron at the hint of a stain. It was part of what made him an outstanding barista.

Buzz, for his part, laced and unlaced his fingers. He paced in his sandals, a tight back-and-forth along the sidewalk. When his phone rang, he'd look at the screen, crossed his arms, and glared at Ryland.

"Ryland," Buzz said. "If you are going to do any accusing, you better do it soon. I've got my lawyer on speed dial, and I have a bomb site where my business used to be. If anyone needs to get on with their day, it's this guy."

"I have a couple questions that only the two of you can answer. If you'd like to call your lawyer, you are welcome to do so at any point. We've not charged anyone with anything."

Elizabeth remembered what Jo said about this being Ryland's first event. He was careful with his words, polished.

The brewer met the deputy's eyes. He put his hands on both hips and pressed his lips into a thin line, then shook his head. "I'm good. For now." There was an unexpected edge to his tone like that of a crisp piece of paper. Ready to cut.

Gary tapped his foot and checked his watch. "Can we please move forward with the questions? I've got a contest to judge. Oh wait, you canceled it. Right. Take as long as you need."

A Sheridan police officer pushed forward, his uniform fresh and unmarked. "Cooperation will help us be as expeditious as possible."

Gary rolled his eyes. "You sound like my second grade teacher."

The other officer wore plain clothes. Instead of a uniform, he'd donned jeans, boots, and a cowboy hat. His badge and the weapon strapped to his belt were the giveaway. *Was he wandering the crowd during the whole fest?*

"Listen, just let us do the directing here," he said, with a wry twist of his lips. "Leave it to the professionals."

Buzz pressed on the officer's patience. "Aren't you the new guy from down south? Do they even have laws down there?"

Down south meant anywhere below the county line. This was an intentional insult, steeped in the history of the Johnson County Wars, and the officer knew it. A southerner couldn't be trusted. Knives couldn't cut the glare between the two men.

"I uphold the law within my jurisdiction regardless of my place of birth, as any quality officer should," Southern said.

Ryland began again. "Mr. Price. You saw the prize money, correct?"

"I did," Gary said.

"Was there anything unusual about it?"

"Andy Jacksons, the whole lot of them. Nothing unusual about that—other than tolerating a slave owner on money in this day and age. Kind of makes you wonder."

Southern said, "Kind of weird they weren't hundos."

"Hang on," Ryland said, scribbling on a notepad. "So, your recollection is that the prize money was in twenty dollar bills?"

"Yep," said Gary. "Looks bigger that way. You know, in a wad."

"If you don't have any questions for me, can I go?"

Ryland turned his attention back to Buzz. "I'm told you had a falling out with our victim, Mr. Gibson."

"She's my former employee. Emphasis on the former."

"I trust that you understand we're just trying to get to the bottom of things."

Buzz sighed. "You and everyone else in town knows she didn't leave on good terms with me. So what?"

"Care to tell us what happened?"

"You know darn well what happened, Deputy. Everyone in town knows!" Buzz's face reddened until he was the shade of a late summer tomato. "She stole from me and sold out to some giant beer maker in Colorado. They churn out my beer by the truckload, and now I can't make it anymore or I'm risking infringement on my own creation."

Gary whistled, a low sound, and shook his head. "What proof do you have?"

"A hat."

29

"HAT?" THE OFFICERS CHIMED in unison. Southern glared at Sheridan.

Elizabeth snickered behind the door, then clapped a hand over her mouth. She slipped farther into the recesses of the entryway and pressed her ear toward the hinge. Leia had long given up on moving to a less cramped spot. She'd curled up on the carpet to start a nap.

Red curtains hung over the door to the janitor's closet. These blocked her from the view of anyone beyond the front doors. To anyone inside the lobby, it would appear as though a well-behaved dog napped near a pair of boots parked below a sheet of crimson velvet.

"Gary, you're the unofficial historian. What getup was Deirdre Sorenson wearing last year at my booth?"

"Ninth year of the festival. We ran the football theme. She came dressed as the World's Biggest Fan."

"Uh huh." Buzz paused for emphasis. "And what was her getup?"

"Cowboys jersey—Laramie, not Dallas. Pigtails, and one of those cheesy hats that hold beer cans and super-long straws."

Southern interrupted the retelling. "The ones that say 'Here for the Beer' on the front?"

"Are there others?"

Southern shrugged, point taken.

"Walk me through how the victim's hat, a style featured in the stands of many NFL games, equals a theft." Sheridan was keeping up, yet skeptical.

Ryland put both hands on his hips and favored his right side. For a moment, she saw him as an Old West gunslinger. In a flash, that picture shifted to one of him playing hopscotch with her kindergarteners. "Not to mention why, to my knowledge, you didn't report this alleged theft."

"He could have come to the city," Sheridan said. Ryland shot him a look.

"I wouldn't," Buzz said. "Y'all are too busy with speeding tickets out in front of the college to deal with actual crime."

It was Sheridan's chance to get huffy.

Ryland waited, the tool of a master. He might have been a greenhorn in the sheriff's department, but he wouldn't fit that bill for too much longer.

"At any rate," Buzz said. "She could have used the straws like siphons to get my beer into the cans, then sealed them up and took them with her."

"That's a pretty big leap for an act you didn't witness," Ryland said, rubbing his chin.

Buzz turned to Gary. "What's the main rule for all competitors when it comes to running their booths?"

"No drinking during the festival," Gary said. Elizabeth mouthed the same words from behind the door.

With Leia lying at her feet, Elizabeth was wedged between an entrance curtain and the door. As if in protest, Leia rolled over and moaned.

"Shhh," Elizabeth whispered.

Southern was weary. Tan lines betrayed more time out of the office than in. A nick at his jawline meant a rushed shave that morning. "So?"

Buzz pulled out his phone. "Check the pictures. Beginning of the day, empty cans in place and dry lines. End of the day, sealed cans and the lines are wet."

Elizabeth wanted to see the group's reaction. In her effort to scoot Leia off the toe of one booth and peer through the crack, she bumped Kevin Costner.

The cutout fell forward and out the doors. It was as though the actor himself had stumbled on the red carpet outside a premiere.

Elizabeth peeked out the door to find five pairs of eyes on her. Leia yelped at the resulting tug on her leash. She'd been dozing, oblivious to the drama.

"I, uh...need to walk my dog." She pointed toward the patch of grass in front of the courthouse.

"No one leaves," said Southern.

"I can do it," offered Sheridan.

"I don't even know you."

Ryland stepped forward to take the leash. "We've got to have folks stay inside. Gary and Buzz here were about to join you. I'll take care of her and bring her back to you, okay?"

Elizabeth gave a slow nod, plan thwarted, and handed over the leash. Leia gave her a baleful look, bothered at her involvement.

Ushered back inside with Gary and Buzz, Elizabeth feigned an excuse for the bathroom. With a glance around for any observers, she ducked into the ticket office.

Elizabeth eased her phone out of her back pocket and tilted the screen away from the big window. A few button presses and the phone rang. The screen light dimmed when pressed against her cheek.

"You'll never guess where I am."

30

"IN A PICKLE."

"A ticket booth-shaped pickle, but yeah."

"Maybe spare me the details. Clint got a call. He's headed in that direction, and I need to act surprised when he gets home tonight. Clint's family is coming into town next week and I'm playing the part of the overly kind wife. I want him to owe me."

"Then I am definitely not hiding from the police in an undisclosed location. How's Rhett?"

There was a rustle against the phone. When Jo returned, she lowered her voice. "He won't leave the nursery. One of the kittens is struggling and he won't leave her side."

Elizabeth's son was born devoted to animals. From the first moment he played with a golden retriever puppy as a nine-month-old, he was smitten. His face lit up with joy as the puppy covered him with kisses. Elizabeth said he learned to crawl to keep up with the pup.

Rhett took longer than most children to begin speaking. Before he started using words, he communicated through his interactions with animals.

Speech wasn't as necessary when she could watch his expressions. He loved all creatures, great and small. It was no surprise to Elizabeth that he would be attached to an ailing animal. That it was a kitten at Corbin's rescue shelter made it a little awkward.

Elizabeth felt an ache knot up, deep within her heart. She wanted to be there with her son, talk with him about the kitten. Take him to see the pig. Not stuck at an unwinnable contest for the foreseeable future with a theater full of increasingly impatient adults.

"I'm trying to coax him out to see the pot bellied pig, but he won't budge."

Outside of his parents and his Uncle Casey, Jo Wolf was Rhett's favorite person. The Blaus' neighbor watched the little boy while Elizabeth was at work.

Jo and Clint had tried for a family but had no kids of their own. Rhett was a balm for Jo's personal heartache.

The two were pals, always on one adventure or another. Their current project involved teaching Rhett to care for her chickens. This included feeding them and collecting eggs. "If you can trust a two-year-old with a fresh egg, you can trust them with a chick," she'd told Elizabeth.

As a bonus, there was no safer daycare than the house of a county sheriff.

Still, Elizabeth missed her son. Constantly. There was no work-life balance when it came to love for your child.

Elizabeth wished work didn't keep her from him so much. There was endless guilt to be found in mothering. She didn't want to miss a moment of his life, yet somehow, it felt as though this was all she did. The fact that she would continue to do so for the rest of her life, ate at her.

"Hey, the feeding timer is going off. I've got to go prep the formula. Pretty sure Rhett will insist on trying the dropper this time. We'll give it a whirl, and I'll get him fed one way or another. I promised Corbin. Have you seen him down there?"

"Yeah," Elizabeth said. "He's here." She debated telling Jo about her failed attempt to ask Corbin out.

"Hang in there. They'll get things moving and you'll be out of there. It's not like it can get much worse."

31

E LIZABETH SLUNK OUT OF the ticket booth. Scoped out the entrance.

The lobby, grand the night of the holiday performance in December, seemed dated and worn. Instead of grandeur, Elizabeth now spotted chips in the paneling. Stains on the carpet. A layer of dust only time could provide coated every surface beyond the reach of a duster. She'd wasted too much time on a hopeless endeavor, and it was as though she felt the wear and tear on herself, as well. It was one thing to trade time with her family for the hope of a better future. It was another to do so for fruitless ambition.

Elizabeth ran a fingertip across the glass counter of the concession stand. She considered her plight. Ryland hadn't said how long he'd be, but Elizabeth was already tired of waiting. Weary of being saddled with a lost cause.

She wasn't alone in that thought. Bored and idle, people wandered in and out of the theater. A few snuck up to the old projection booth to check out the mechanics. Water cups were strewn about below the dispenser. The lines for the restrooms grew as patience among the crowd ran short.

Elizabeth parted the curtains to the theater itself. The thick drapery blocked the seats from the sounds of the lobby. She stood at the top of the main aisle, the carpeted floor angling down toward the stage. Inside, people sprawled in all manner of positions. Across the chairs, in the middle of the aisles, along the walls. Otis and Judy sat on the edge of the stage in quiet discussion. A few others sat on the steps at stage left.

A football zinged across the seats as a rowdy group tossed it back and forth across the venue. Low tones of conversation drifted along those gathered. Occasional shouts punctuated the din.

Elizabeth pursed her lips and huffed. "Is anyone in charge of this circus?"

She hadn't realized the words had left her lips until she heard her brother reply.

"Liz," Casey said. His head popped up from the first few rows of seats. "Where've you been?"

Casey heaved himself up from the recesses of the velvety plushness. He swung his legs over first one row and then another to make his way to the aisle. "Any news?

Elizabeth met him in the middle of the theater. "You know as much as I do. And what I know can fit on the end of Leia's nose. What are we supposed to do?"

"What can we do? Ryland said to wait here."

Elizabeth shook her head. "I don't want to wait here. I wanted to win, and now that I can't, I just want to go home." Elizabeth crossed her arms and plunked down in the nearest seat to pout.

A flash of turquoise popped against the dark interior and caught Elizabeth's attention. She looked up.

The WYO Theater had twin balconies. Each flanked the projection booth. A couple dozen seats lined up like soldiers. It was their contents that dropped Elizabeth's heart into her gut.

In the second to the last row of the upper right hand side, Corbin lounged, relaxed, his bright blue jacket draped over an adjacent seat. One ankle hooked over the back of the row in front of him. One arm looped over the shoulders of a woman Elizabeth knew all too well.

32

H ANNAH BLACK.

Elizabeth pressed her lips into a thin line and puffed out her cheeks. How could this day sink further into the pits?

"Liz? Lizzie-Beth? Oh, sister of mine—are you in there?" Casey waved a hand in front of her face.

"Huh? Oh. What was that?"

"I said, your phone is ringing."

A muted chirping escaped Elizabeth's back pocket. She fumbled with the device in her rush to answer. "Hello?"

"Hey, it's Titus from Bone Brews. Now an okay time to talk?

On a run up to Billings for supplies, Elizabeth had stopped in a few local breweries. Titus had been easy to talk to, interested in her process and her style. He said he'd let her know if there were any opportunities for her. "Now is all we ever have. I mean to say, that the now we just had is gone, and there is a new one, now. And there it goes again. In fact, the average human will experience over two to three billion nows in their lifetime—assuming each one is about a second long."

Casey watched his sister, brows lifted, quizzical.

Titus chuckled. "You were right, trivia is your forte. Listen, I talked with our roaster, and he is interested in working with you. We're wondering if you could come up here for some sampling. Bring some of your beers. We can sort out a profile, what kind of collaboration might work out."

"That's great! Really great. I would love to. What's the timeline?" When Casey made faces at her—puffing out his cheeks and pulling on his ears in a warped monkey face—she rotated away from him to focus on the conversation.

"Here's the thing. We've had a few other brewers reach out with interesting distribution options. We need to make a decision. Go with the best fit for our brand. Can you get something for us next week?"

Elizabeth's joy sank, pooling at her feet. She thought of the stout, unfinished in the barn. The beers she'd brought to this event, wasted on a canceled contest. Prize money that would have meant more ingredients and equipment. Upgrades that meant she could run more varieties.

"That quick?"

"If it's too soon, we can put you on the list for next year's spots."

Elizabeth thought of the sacrifices she'd made up until this moment. The late nights brewing, tasting, and dreaming. Outlining a business plan with her brother. Phone calls to the best coffee shops to find one that would work with her. One that did its own roasting and used fair trade coffee. Exhausting herself at her day job, reading picture books all day to other people's kids only to come home too tired to do the same for her own son. She couldn't find the energy to start over, again.

"I...I'm not sure I'll be able to make that timeline. I'll try."

"Ah, okay. If something changes, let us know. We loved the whole single-mom brewer thing and wanted to make sure we gave you a solid shot."

"Thank you," Elizabeth said. "I'll be in touch." She hung up the phone and collapsed into the nearest seat. The metal springs squeaked in protest from within.

"Who is Bone Brews?"

"Only one of the top breweries in Billings, that's who. Happens to be right next door to the best coffee shop, too. They want me to audition my beers for a collaboration. This would be fantastic except that I don't have a variety of quality beer available. I brought the best of what I had to this contest. I don't know how long it will take to recreate what I made. Definitely not a week."

"Oh, sis," Casey said. "I'm sorry."

Elizabeth pressed her face into her hands. "They are willing to consider me again...next year." Her carefully scheduled plan for resuscitating her brewing career crumbled in front of her eyes. She squeezed them shut against the news. "So much for business ownership. Guess I'm back to the hobby level."

Casey waited, silent, as Elizabeth fought back tears. When he reached out to squeeze her shoulder, she flinched away from him. "I'm going to get some air."

Elizabeth shoved at the curtains to the lobby. Halfway to the front door, she remembered their locked-in status. When she spun around to seek a bathroom stall in which to cry, she ran smack into Corbin.

"Are you okay?" he asked, holding her out at arms' length until she could steady herself.

Elizabeth couldn't meet his eyes.

"So, Hannah is your old friend," she said to the floor. She remembered a photograph of the two of them she'd found in Casey's office that winter.

Hannah's estranged husband had fallen to his death when his brother pushed him off a cliff face last December. She was now a wealthy widow, with an even bigger stake in the family sled dog business. She'd donated the land for Corbin's new shelter facility. Elizabeth could connect the dots to the rekindling of an old romance.

Corbin ran a hand across the back of his head. Looked down at the floor. "Uh, yeah. Something like that."

"I didn't even think she liked dogs. Let alone llamas and goats."

Realization tugged at the corners of Corbin's mouth. "When she helped out Burro Buddies, we reconnected," he said. "The animals are growing on her."

"Got it," Elizabeth said. With a shallow smile and a brief nod, she headed back into the theater, the only escape.

Casey was near the entrance. He rested his crossed arms on the back of a seat in front of him. Deep in an animated conversation with Danny, he didn't see her.

Danny held a mile-wide grin while Casey talked. When her brother finished telling a story, Danny laughed a big, booming burst of joy. He put his hand on Casey's arm for the briefest of moments.

Could he be interested in Casey—and single?

Elizabeth wanted to be happy for her brother. Instead, sourness flooded her senses. Had she had her own shot at happiness?

There wasn't a soul who could talk her back into a life with Nick. She could love the father he was becoming for her son while being happy she was no longer his wife.

But she was...alone.

While she felt the ache of a blemished reality, it was at least an authentic one. Forced allegiance to a lie only made people miserable, resentful. Still, in darker moments, she wondered if it was just her and Rhett from here on out.

And Casey. And Jo and Clint. She was hardly alone, hardly unhappy. *Come on, Liz. No pity parties.*

And Leia. *Where is Ryland with my dog?*

33

B EER PONG STARTED UP in the long hall. A folding table wrestled out from inside the broom closet was the roost for cups of water borrowed from the concession stand. Without access to the beers, players kept track of the shots owed on an old movie poster. Tally marks filled the border of the image.

Rebellion flooded her veins. If they were going to be stuck inside, why couldn't they be stuck inside *with* beer? The only things keeping them from continuing the contest were the lack of product and missing prize money. They could get the beer. She'd worry about the second problem later.

At the front doors, Elizabeth looked over her shoulder into the lobby. No one paid the slightest notice. She angled Costner to block the view of her escape attempt.

Her toes just inside the threshold, Elizabeth cracked the front door open. She could see the street corner but not much else without violating Ryland's command. Around the corner, she heard the goats bleat. Corbin would have provided water and food, but idle farm animals could spell trouble. Irritated without the streaming line of treats and people to watch, it was a matter of time before they attempted destruction. Perhaps she could sneak them a cracker—or two. With a shove, she levered the door all the way open, then recoiled.

Sheridan and Southern, arms folded, braced for her escape, their backs to Main. Matching aviators shrouded their expressions. Each wore polished shoes despite the differences in uniform.

Southern had a five o'clock shadow. Bristles dusted his jaw. In contrast, Sheridan was a blond, mustached, with a tiny fish tattooed at his wrist. Identical boots and frowns cataloged her every move. Bookends and bouncers, Elizabeth wouldn't be going anywhere.

Behind them, the tents flapped. Crumpled tasting notes sheets flipped across the pavement, caught in the breeze. The once bustling street festival was empty. Meanwhile, dozens of jockey boxes waited to be tapped, the beer warming in the afternoon heat.

Sheridan cleared his throat when she ventured a foot onto the sidewalk.

"I'm looking for my dog," she said. Elizabeth injected her tone with every ounce of irritation from her interaction with Corbin. She'd bottled it, saving the ire for such a moment. "As soon as I get her back, you're going to help me bring all this beer inside so we can get on with the contest."

"Deputy Ryland ordered everyone to stay put. We will begin—"

"Mayor Roberts made it clear that the contest is—"

"Yeah, yeah," she said, icicles dangling from her words. "So you said. So I've heard. Yet here we still are with absolutely nothing happening, and I'm being deprived of my dog and my win. Come with me if you want," she said, stepping out from the doors. "I'm going to look for Ryland, and then we're going to get this event back in gear."

"You're looking for me? Here's Leia, all sorted," Ryland said. He had Leia's leash in one hand, his radio in the other.

"Thanks," Elizabeth said. "If only I could say that for the rest of us." A flash of a grimace crossed Ryland's face. She added, "Sorry, that was rude. I think I'm a bit on edge. Rather, we're all a little on edge."

"An understatement if ever there was one," he said. With a nod, Ryland turned to walk away. Garbled voices over his radio asked at what point he would want to begin searching the booths.

Before Ryland could take five steps, two events happened at once.

Elizabeth needed Ryland's buy-in for the next phase of her plan. She stepped forward to tap the shoulder of his retreating form when her foot crunched something underfoot.

At the same moment, glass exploded from the windows of Maximum Brewing before a ball of fire burst out of the roof.

34

A BODY IS A *heavy thing.*

Don't get me wrong, one hundred and sixty pounds is the same weight whether it's in bags of barley, a full keg, or a human being.

I took science like everyone else. Weight is weight.

It's just that this isn't something you plan to know. Plan to experience.

Hoisting her over my shoulder wasn't an option. Too much contact. I'd seen enough TV.

I didn't want to touch her more than I had to—good thing we all were wearing gloves.

No one thinks twice about where cardboard boxes come from. Where they go. As long as your recycling gets picked up each week like clockwork, you never stop to think about what happens to it, do you? You don't. So, spare me your judgment for using the big screen TV box you didn't think twice about tossing into the alley for someone else to deal with.

Technically, I did reuse it. One side got a little beat up along the asphalt. It's not like you were going to keep it.

Enjoying that TV now?

I mean, it's not like I started my week thinking, "Better pick up the groceries, reattach the gutters, and figure out how I'm going to handle a dead body."

In a typical week, I like beer like the next person. Trail rides. Motorcycle magazines.

There's what you set out to do with your time and what life hands off. I've learned that some weeks, it's a leaky faucet, other times, it's the body of someone you used to know.

Makes it easier to handle a body. The part where you used to know them. Only way it could be easier is if it was a stranger. Then again, if it was a stranger, I would have been less freaked about the whole thing. Less pressed to find a spot.

Location is everything, let me tell you.

I couldn't leave her anywhere that would point fingers my way. That was my immediate thought.

Dragging could only be a short-distance option. A crowded place meant too many ideas to get away with much for long.

I had a tiny pocket of time to cover up. Being on the lookout was an unexpected thrill.

Then came the woman and the dog.

In another time, or maybe a year from now, she would have been my type. Taller, great biceps, and a no-nonsense wardrobe that said, "I work for a living." Someone who looked earnest. Like your favorite horse.

That's the kind of girl I want around. One who could be loyal, dedicated to the craft, and easy to have around the place. A cute dog is a bonus. A mascot.

She was looking for something. Her car, a grassy spot for the pooch, or the meaning of life, I don't know. What I am sure of is that she had a lot going on in her head. You can tell that about people. When they are moving but aren't responsive. There's a vacant look in their eyes, and the only thing they see is the memories playing in the back of their mind. We've all had those moments. You get super bad—or good—news, and it's like the rest of the world fades into the background while you think through whatever ghosts are on your tail.

I've been her. You've been her. That's what unites us.

I'm told dogs are the best companions for those times. Happy to heel, speak, and beg, while you bear the weight of the world on your shoulders.

Always been a cat person myself.

The two of them were there, and then they were gone, back into the crowd.

Speaking of weight. Dead weight.

We'd been a team. Had plans. So much for that.
I had to work with what I had. And fast.
Risking my future—again—was not an option.
Choices were made.
The explosion was icing on the cake.

35

C HAPTER THIRTY-FIVE

The world rushed in around Elizabeth, a tornado of action.

Leia flattened herself against the sidewalk, her legs locked, two loops of nylon leash wrapped around Elizabeth's waist. The dog popped her head between Elizabeth's ankles, seeking shelter in the madness.

Sheridan and Southern took off toward the building. Each ran like it was Mile Day in middle school PE. Boot soles slapped at the ground. Shoulders flung back, arms pumping. Feet pounded the pavement in rapid rhythm.

Within seconds, they were in front of the brewery. Panting.

Sheridan went right, Southern went left. Southern hop-skipped over a hunk of metal, chunks of glass. Sheridan was slower, circling remnants that littered the sidewalk. The pair made a visual assessment, checked the damage for people to help. More danger, new destruction.

Ryland's mouth hung agape for exactly four seconds. After a brief shake of his head, he was back. His left hand flew to the radio on his right shoulder. He spouted commands into its speaker. When a reply came through, he took off after the other two officers.

Pedestrians who'd been near the explosion had collapsed on the sidewalk. A mother checked over every inch of her daughter for shrapnel. She'd thrown herself over her child, though the mailbox blocked the two from much of the flying debris.

One man removed a shoe to examine a shard of glass wedged in the exterior. His face was ashen. Dust settled on his shoulders. Ashen snow.

Some who'd been nearby rushed over to help. Several others cowered under the awning of a printer shop next door, uncertain. Elizabeth heard people yelling for 911 and for a nurse in the crowd. The wail of an ambulance was audible in the distance.

People jostled out of the theater doors only to freeze outside the threshold. Eyes wide. Many covered their ears. Most took out their phones to snap pictures, call friends.

Unsure whether the latest emergency signaled the freedom to leave, people teetered at the entrance. A repeat of the question of whether or stay or go uttered throughout the group. Everyone asked, no one answered. Ripples of information rolled through the crowd. Some whispered, others shouted. Controlled chaos bounced among them like a pinball machine.

From somewhere over Elizabeth's shoulder, she heard her brother's disembodied voice. "Well, this party sure got a lot more complicated."

Elizabeth stood in the eye, a quiet focal point. She lifted first the heel, then the ball of her foot, inching up from the sidewalk as though a sloth were her puppeteer.

Under her heel was a mangled mess of metal and tiny beads. Like stars scattered across the night sky, the minuscule decorations formed constellations on the blacktop.

Elizabeth squatted low to examine the pieces. She scooped the bits into her hand. Fine white threads held some of the beads to a thin strip of leather.

Fire trucks joined the ambulance. Firefighters scrambled down from the vehicles. They went to work hauling a hose toward the nearest hydrant. Elizabeth was shoved forward as a few of the firefighters who'd been off duty at the festival rushed out to assist.

With her thumb, she pressed on the beads still attached to the leather. They formed the start of a pattern, stripes across the thin strip of hide. The metal pieces, about the length of her hand, ended in a clasp.

"A barrette," she said to no one, though both Leia and Casey looked her way.

Casey looked over her shoulder at the handful of what was once a hair accessory. "You okay? Did you see what happened?"

Elizabeth mulled over the barrette. *Crow*, she ventured. The reservation, the largest in the state, was over the border in Montana. This was the type of item sold in the shops along the highway to drive-through tourists. Something about the pattern, black, red, and yellow stripes, nagged at her mind.

There'd been an explosion, after a potential murder, and her response was to fixate on a barrette.

Elizabeth had forgotten the heart of the day, the purpose for the gathering.

"Hey—hello in there." Casey stepped in front of his sister and gave her forearm a squeeze. "How close were you when this happened? Are you okay? Liz, I swear, if you don't start making sense, I'm dragging you over to the paramedics. Maybe you need a once over. And heck, depending on which ones show up, I might need a once over."

Elizabeth looked at her brother as though she saw him for the first time that day.

"I've got an idea. You're going to help me pull it off."

36

C HAPTER THIRTY-SIX

"I'm all ears."

"Good. Step one, find that cutie with the forest beer. The Swede."

"Danny?"

"Yep, we're going to need him."

"Aye, aye, captain." Casey saluted and took off at a jog.

Elizabeth turned her back to the chaos in the street behind her. She swished her hands in front of her to shoo the audience. "Back inside, y'all. Let the professionals sort this out. The deputy expects us to be here and waiting when he gets back from that mess."

A testy bartender stood his ground. "Why do you get to tell us what to do? You're not even from here." He held his hands clasped in front of himself, feet planted. His shirt labeled him as *Hoptimist*.

Elizabeth approached the man until she stood toe to toe with him. She looked up to the base of his chin. "None of us are from here. You are going to tell me your ancestors have never lived anywhere else?" The man broke eye contact and she continued, "This mom wants to get home to her son. The fastest way for me to do that is to do what I'm told and encourage others to do the same. Can you get that through your thick head?"

The man said nothing. He pushed a wad of tobacco from one corner of his mouth across his teeth to the other side. Elizabeth bit back her nausea at the smell of his breath.

"Well, can you? The rest of us would like to get back to the contest."

This caught the man by surprise. "The contest is back on?"

"It will be if we work together."

He shifted from one foot to the other. Pressed the tobacco wad to the other side of his mouth. "All right. I'm listening."

"We have the beer. We have taste testers. We have judges. What more do we need?"

Casey returned with Danny. Elizabeth explained the finer details of her plan to the three men.

The tobacco man nodded, the slow confirmation of a dog whose bark is worse than his bite. "I'll get some guys to move stuff. Get things set up in here. Leave the tables to me." He disappeared into the theater.

Elizabeth spotted a festival poster stuck to the wall. "The tenth annual Tap Fest isn't going down without a fight."

Gary joined her near the doorway. "Big Ricky in there told me some unbalanced woman out front had a plan to salvage this train wreck. Said he was going to get the folding tables set up while she sorted out some harebrained idea. Should have guessed he meant the ever-savvy Elizabeth Blau. How can I help?"

Elizabeth grinned. "Gary, can you collect the ballot chip boxes from the tables? We'll need to redistribute those in a fair way once we have everyone set up again."

"I'm on it," he said. "Wait, aren't we going to get barked at for going outside?"

"Let me handle that. I think if we're quick, they won't see much, if anything, of our temporary escape."

Gary gave Elizabeth a high-five and was out the door to the abandoned booths.

"Okay," Elizabeth said to her brother and Danny. "I need you two to bring in all the jockey box setups. Figure out the table arrangement with Big Ricky. Go get the beer, one booth at a time. Reunite people with their taps."

"What about me?" James piped up from behind. "I'm here to help."

Elizabeth considered the assistant. "Are you familiar with the sound system?"

James considered. "No, but I could figure it out. They've all got the same bones."

"Awesome. Get it sorted, then let me know. We can't give people the new rundown without some proper amplification."

"Your wish is my command." James saluted Elizabeth and was off.

Elizabeth directed her next comment to the dog at her feet. "Okay, girl. We're on door duty."

For the next half hour, the small but mighty crew moved the bulk of the festival inside.

Big Ricky lined the lobby and the edge of the theater with folding tables. They made a neat loop a taster could follow on the quest to try all the beers.

Gary had the contestants sorted among the tables. He ushered brewers to their new table before he handed each their ballot bucket.

Separated from their original decorations, some people became creative. Bandanas served as makeshift placemats. Folded paper flowers lined the tabletops.

Casey and Danny hauled the beer-based contents of each booth to its new location indoors. Elizabeth waited by the doors to swing them wide open upon their approach. She caught snippets of their conversation each time they passed. They'd gone from debating a proper pale ale to listing their top five favorite breweries. Casey detailed his plans for a new goat cheese variety whipped with honey. Danny clung to his every word.

Before the officers could object, the small team turned the theater into a proper beer hall.

"This could actually work," Big Ricky said. Hands on hips, he surveyed the set up. "We ought to go into business!"

"Doing what?" Elizabeth unfolded two metal chairs and plunked them behind a table. "Weddings and family reunions?"

Gary joined them. "How about solving murders?"

37

"MURDERS?" ELIZABETH HEADED DOWN the aisle toward the stage, Gary in tow.

"Seems like that's all you've done since you moved here. Since we may have one on our hands again, it's a good thing you're here."

"Why, are you a suspect?"

Gary caught up with Elizabeth. "That's what the two knuckle-draggers suggested out front. Grilled Buzz and I like we were on TV."

"I get that Buzz knew her, but why you?"

"You think Buzz is a murderer?"

Chatter at the tables that ringed the room rose to a steady hum. As brewers prepared to again welcome the thirsty, attendees watched from the theater seats. Anticipation flowed through the room. The energy was catching.

"I don't even know the man. I'm surprised about you is all." It's true, she didn't know Buzz. She did know a venomous tone when she heard it, though. That wasn't Gary's style.

Gary shrugged. "We had a meeting before things kicked off. All the judges. Deirdre didn't like what I had to say. We argued about voting. She thought only judges should cast votes. Mayor Roberts must have told Tweedle Dee and Tweedle Dum about it. They told Ryland."

Elizabeth spun to face Gary. "What did you say to her?"

Gary looked at his feet. "I may have told her that if she did anything shady this year, she'd pay for it."

Elizabeth's eyebrows shot up. "Bold statement."

Gary was the ersatz keeper of secrets in Sheridan County. His placement as barista at one of the two coffee shops meant he heard an earful every day. The job came with listening to the theatrics of customers, much like a hair stylist or bartender.

"Drama comes from people not satisfied with their lot," he said. "That woman created nothing but trouble when she left. Lit every metaphorical bridge in the tri-county area aflame on her way out of town. Even if the rumors aren't true about what she did, she was awful. Blamed everything on this tiny "zit on the prairie" for holding her back. I tell you what, if there's one thing that gets people upset out here, it's when you talk trash about our little haven."

"I've picked up as much myself."

"If she had any plans to cause problems, I wanted them squashed. The only reason she was invited back is that she is—was—Danny Sorenson's cousin. Didn't feel right to throw a celebration in honor of their family and not let her attend. Especially since she does—or rather, did—work for a legitimate brewer. The planning committee thought she might have changed. Missed her roots. When it came to giving her a second shot, I was outvoted."

"What would have been the harm in letting her come?"

Gary gestured to the haphazard setup surrounding them. "Besides all this?"

"Come on, it's not like she planned to die here."

He sighed and sucked in his lower lip. "It might have been fine. She might have behaved herself. Used her fancy Fort Collins knowledge as a judge. Reconnected with some old friends—if she had any left. Then gone home. That didn't happen."

"No, it didn't. But now we have a Tap Fest to relaunch. So, if you could kindly hop on stage and make the announcement, the tide will start to shift. The mayor is MIA, and people are getting antsy."

Elizabeth had watched the guests catch wind of what the brewers were doing. A few pressed toward the end of the aisles. Some formed a pre-line in front of Danny's table, in case the rumors were true.

He and Casey had made quick work of delivering coolers to their rightful brewers. They'd stacked the boxes of mugs in the center aisle. Casey had changed out the water cooler jug. Danny had even dragged in one of his stumps. Elizabeth hoped her brother had taken the chance to bring in some of their food storage.

If the contest was back on, she needed to get back into competition mode.

James appeared at Gary's side as he mounted the short flight of steps. The assistant hovered around the venue like a dragonfly. Flitted between tables and landed for only a moment before taking off again. He fussed with the mic stand before uttering "check, check" into the device. With a nod, he handed the microphone to Gary and stepped back, hands clasped in front of himself.

"Excuse me folks," Gary said. The crowd hushed across the facility.

Sound systems in theaters were more than the electronics. They were the shape of the walls, the slope of the floor. The right combination maximized the sound of a pin drop.

Gary's voice traveled the length and depth of the seats. "Taps will reopen in ten minutes, at 5:30 on the nose. If you don't still have your mug, you can get one out of the boxes. You still have time to cast your votes. While the prize money is gone,"—a few gasps in the crowd interrupted his speech—"we will still have our grand prize winner, so every vote counts. Please be kind to our brewers. They've gone the extra mile for us all. Without further ado, Prost!"

Gary thrust his mug up in the air. The gesture echoed around the room and a few toasted. People dug taster coins from inside their pockets. They shuffled up and down aisles to be the first in line for the beers they'd missed.

At the Blau booth, Casey had reassembled the two trays of snacks in front of the beers.

"Looking good. We just might have a chance."

Casey grimaced. "Glad you think so. We still don't have ice. I plugged in the theater ice maker, but that could take a while."

"Can we get our hands on any? Even dry ice?" As a chemistry teacher, Elizabeth loved frozen carbon dioxide. Easy enough to store, lasted longer, and made a cool mist students loved to see.

"When the officers get back, I'll ask. I'm hoping to buy a favor with their joy at my finding a way to get this ship back on course."

"Keep the drunks occupied? Good because all eyes are on you."

"I think they're all on Danny. Look at that line."

Danny Sorenson had a queue of people running down the row in front of his table and into the aisle.

"I'm getting that ice. Can't let a lumberjack show us up."

38

POINTER FINGERS ARE BEST for a tap on the shoulder. Firm enough to command attention, light enough to seem conversational.

Ryland whirled at Elizabeth's touch.

"I need ice."

"Ms. Blau." Ryland paused against the wall outside the manager's office. "I see. How can I assist?"

Two attendees sat in chairs outside the office door. One scrolled on his phone. The other crossed and uncrossed her ankles while she nibbled at her cuticles.

"This is a rather unorthodox interview room."

Ryland wiped his hand across his mouth. "We aren't exactly operating in ideal conditions."

"We need to keep the food cold. Only so much to go around."

"I see. And the machine?"

Elizabeth appealed to his sense of reason. "Running, but not fast enough to keep up. Take me to the beermobile, so I can get some for all of us."

Ryland shook his head. "No can do. We're deep in interviews."

"Oh, come on. Look at these two. They're not going anywhere."

The pair on deck volleyed their eyes between each other and the deputy.

Sheridan opened the door and released the mayor.

"Mayor Roberts," Ryland said, and doffed his hat.

"Deputy." After a nod, the official turned back to shake hands with Sheridan. "I would appreciate a swift end to this investigation, officers. The townspeople would appreciate returning to their lives as soon as possible."

"About that," Elizabeth said. "We've had some developments."

Five pairs of eyes looked her way. Southern poked his head out from inside the office to join them.

"Developments?"

"Everyone is perfectly happy. Jolly, even. You see, we got the contest up and running again. Take a look."

The three lawmen, one judge, and two attendees shuffled over to the projection booth. Through the opening, they peered down on the theater. Lively chatter rose up from the seats. People waited in lines, lounged in seats, and clustered in groups. Laughter bubbled up from the gathering.

Ryland whistled. "Well I'll be."

The mayor blinked. "Guess I'll get back to judging."

"About that ice—"

With his pointer finger, Ryland beckoned the phone scroller into the office. "All right, I've got to get the next person from downstairs anyway. Five minutes."

On the sidewalk, Elizabeth squinted into the late afternoon rays of sunlight. "This way."

She led Ryland through the abandoned booths toward the beermobile. "They had a few coolers full. Plenty to share."

The deputy ducked under the canvas flaps on the tents. His height made life a constant obstacle course. "How did you get everyone organized? They were bickering like cats and dogs before the explosion."

Elizabeth hopped over a fallen chair back. "Is that what happened? I saw an opportunity and took it, is all. Like Ben Franklin said, 'God intended beer for our enjoyment.'"

The beermobile loomed in front of them, its metal ramp extended and a hand truck tipped against the side.

Ryland took hold of the handle on the back door and jerked. The door didn't budge. "Locked?"

"There's a trick to it," Elizabeth said. She gave the door a swift kick. Metal plinked against metal. She lifted the back handle, and the door rolled up and out of the way. "The pin sticks."

"On a normal day, I'd be suspicious of anyone who knows how to break into another person's vehicle. This day ain't close to normal."

Elizabeth dragged a foam cooler forward and peeked inside. Satisfied, she set it on the ground and reached for another. "I like details, deputy, that's all."

"I've noticed," Ryland said. He stacked the first two coolers.

"Like dry ice. Solid carbon dioxide. Goes straight from that solid to gas. A process called sublimation. Unlike water ice, it sinks. Lasts longer, doesn't get everything wet." Elizabeth threw her body forward into the truck to grab the last two coolers. She heaved them out. "Lighter, too. Thank goodness."

Ryland opened one cooler to peer inside. "Clint said you were a high school science teacher. How'd you end up with the littles?"

"Still am a science teacher. Can't stop being something you love just because life takes you in a different direction. Starting earlier with the students, that's all."

Ryland hefted the two coolers onto the hand truck, then added a third. "I need to thank you."

"For the science lesson?"

"For fixing the beer fest."

Elizabeth lifted the last cooler and shrugged. "Organizing people is something I do in my day job."

She didn't mention how much she wanted to win the contest, could taste the celebration. To do so would admit her desire to someone else, a risky move if in the end she lost. Defeat was easier to swallow alone. She started toward the theater but stopped when the sound of squeaky wheels didn't follow. Cooler in hand, Elizabeth faced him.

Ryland scrutinized her. "Not just anyone would do that, you know. Could do that, even. Helped us out. Folks will be happier to wait around a bit longer. Looser-lipped, too."

Elizabeth laughed. "That part was not my intention."

Ryland smiled. "Still."

"Come on, deputy. I've got beer to keep cold, and you've got a murder to solve."

39

*P*LINK. PLUNK.

The sound of voting chips bouncing off others in their bucket gave Elizabeth a tiny burst of joy.

She nudged Casey in between pours. Their line was steady. "I think we're doing really well. We've got a few dozen at least. People are going nuts for these pairings."

"So, you're saying I was right. Can I get this in writing? I need to record it for posterity."

"Very funny," said Elizabeth. "You were right, and I didn't know what I was talking about."

"Thank you," said Casey.

They had their operation down pat. Casey would ask each beer drinker which pairing they would like. He would then hand them a loaded napkin while Elizabeth filled their mug to the sample line. This way, they kept the line moving and the customers happy.

Since Gary officially opened the taps for business, the mood had lifted in the theater. It was as though he'd restarted an engine. Elizabeth wondered if that was part beer fest, part people making the best of the situation. The Blau table was hopping.

"Are you all available for parties?" One woman whipped out her phone to check a calendar. "I've got to host a thing at the office."

A real estate agent also wanted their contact information. "What about catering events? I'm having a little get together, and I would love to have a tasting experience."

Casey had long since exhausted the supply of business cards. Elizabeth borrowed blank tickets from the lobby machine out of desperation. She scrawled contact information on the backs to hand out to anyone without a phone.

Elizabeth jotted names and phone numbers of those they met on the back of a beer splattered page in her planner. She made notes of timelines, menu interests, and themes. There was the real estate office opening, the dinner party, and a girls' weekend. She and Casey had the potential to book quite a few social events.

A newfound reality took shape, separate from winning the Tap Fest. What if her avenue to success was through a partnership with her brother? She could have greater control over her products. If she worked with or for a brewery, they might want change or compromise. Little by little, a Plan B simmered at the back of her mind.

Elizabeth looked up to the projection booth. She knew this new festival format would last only as long as their confinement. The interviews progressed, one by one. Every few minutes, someone would descend the steps back into the gathering. Friends would circle them, and a hushed conversation would follow. Another would take their place in the office. A grim assembly line.

Elizabeth caught snippets of talk as folks passed the table.

"I told them I didn't see anything because I didn't. Don't know who did, but they'll find 'em."

"Do you think she saw it coming? Or someone snuck up on her?"

"Told the deputy I hadn't seen her in over a year. Maybe longer. He's up to his knees in it for sure with this one."

"Someone will crack. They just need one good tip. Sheriff won't be too happy if they foul this up."

"We may have struck gold," Casey said.

"Huh?" Eavesdropping hijacked her focus.

Elizabeth switched gears back over to their sudden success.

"I've been thinking about what this could look like. Even if we land only a few of these parties," Casey said, excitement written all over his face. "We've got something unique. Classy.

And I've already got a client list that will spread the word about our products."

To launch his goat cheese business, Casey had relied on his interior design clientele. He'd decorated more high-end ranch houses in the county than he could count. These customers had deep pockets as did their social circles.

Elizabeth was silent, thinking. To hear him say what she'd already been considering made it all so real, legitimate. Being in control of future potential felt good. Really good.

A moment later, guilt darkened her glee.

"What's that face? See, this is why you can't play poker. Anyone would know what you're holding."

"I'm totally happy. I am. It's just...I don't know. Maybe feeling a little bad? There's a murder investigation going on here. Someone died. Meanwhile, I want to jump up and down and shout over all the good things happening. Feels kind of wrong."

"I can't be sure," Casey said. "But I will say that this goodness would have happened, murder or not. Don't get me wrong, we're going to remember this Tap Fest for one big horrific reason. I'm hoping we also remember it as the launch of something big for us."

Elizabeth knew he was right, but there was still a knot in the pit of her stomach. That a door opened for her the day it closed for someone else may have been the way of life, but it was unsettling.

She needed it to be tomorrow, for them to be home. With space and time to think and plan.

Lights above them flickered throughout the theater, then dimmed.

What is happening?

A beam from the projector booth shot forth, aimed for the giant screen. Shuffling and a swear or two could be heard from the booth overhead. With a burst of sound and projection, a train careened around the track on the giant screen. "Scenes from Bavaria" scrolled across the screen along with opening credits. Cheers erupted from the booth.

People navigated the rows to take seats while they sipped. The train wound its way through gorgeous mountain ranges and alongside pristine lakes. The footage was a few decades old, but the content was timeless. Someone had dug an oldie but a goodie out of storage.

Bavaria. Germany. Elizabeth tumbled those words in her mind like rocks in need of a polish.

"Ms. Blau?"

Deputy Ryland stood at their booth, a clipboard in hand.

"My turn? Give me just a sec," she said, and untied her apron.

"Not just yet," Ryland said. "I did have a question for you, though. Can I borrow you for a moment?"

Casey raised an eyebrow and nodded. Elizabeth followed the deputy toward the lobby.

Ryland gestured toward the ticket booth. "In there, okay?"

Elizabeth followed him inside. What had worked for her phone call, ducked down below the window, was tight quarters for two people.

"Could you take a look at these numbers and tell me if they mean anything to you?"

She was almost nose to nose with the deputy. Coffee, she thought, smelling his breath. Dark roast.

Ryland handed over the clipboard. On it was a photograph of a document. Handwriting in blue ink covered the page. Letters, numbers, and symbols. The strokes were quick and light, as though speed were a component of the notetaking.

"Kind of looks like some science to me," he said. "You know, chemistry. Where we talk about elements and formulas, and all that, but it's been a few years. I figured you would know if there's anything to it."

Elizabeth ran through her mental catalog of elements and formulas.

She gave a slow shake of her head. "Doesn't look like anything I remember. Granted, I don't know *every* molecular formula."

"Shoot, I was hoping it was something."

"I'm pretty sure it's not. See the Js? No elements use the letter J in their symbol."

Ryland's shoulders slumped. "All right. Back to the drawing board. Thanks for your help."

"Where did you find this?"

"The sheet slipped out from our victim's...er...upper clothing. When they moved her."

40

"I T WAS IN HER *bra?*" Casey was dubious.

"He didn't exactly say that in so many words. But I got the message."

"Bizarre. Like she was a secret spy."

Elizabeth shrugged. "Or her dress didn't come with pockets."

While she considered Ryland's find, she ran her fingers across what was left of the beaded barrette.

During the chaos of the explosion, she'd slipped the remnants into her pocket. To discard the intricate, detailed, beautiful piece seemed cruel. Disrespectful.

There was something she needed to figure out before she tossed it. A detail that called to her. If she could find the barrette's owner, she could find the answer.

Ryland had headed back up the stairs, two at a time, to check in on the interviews. He promised to take Leia out for a break in the next hour.

For now, her dog enjoyed the crowd's adoration. Leia sprawled in front of the booth, tongue lolling. Big brown, puppy-like eyes solicited pets from everyone who passed their table. Everyone who stopped asked her name and origin.

"She's a Chinook dog. About three, we think."

Elizabeth had requested Leia's paperwork from her former owner, Hannah Black. There didn't seem to be any urgency to fulfill that request.

"Never heard of them."

"Out of New Hampshire. It's a very cool story. Super rare breed. Bred to be the ultimate sled dog. Great with kids. My son's best friend."

"I'll check them out. New Hampshire, you say?"

This conversation repeated with almost every beer drinker who stopped by. Most would ask if they could offer Leia a cookie.

"That dog is going to have a tummy ache if this keeps up," Casey said.

"Ryland said he'd take her out soon. Maybe I should walk her around a bit? Get some fresh water."

Elizabeth collected both the dog and bowl and started up the aisle for the lobby. There was a small sink behind the concession stand counter.

"There's my top competitor," Danny called from his table. "Was wondering if you'd given up."

Danny filled two more mugs, then mopped his brow with a dish towel. He flipped the towel back over his shoulder and returned to his taps.

"The heat of our presence getting to you, Sorenson?"

Danny smiled. "No, ma'am. It's that I haven't stopped pouring since Gary opened the floodgates."

Elizabeth watched as he pulled a perfect mug for an eager patron. Pale and golden, a thin head. "I'll admit, that does look like a good ale."

Danny passed the mug to its owner. The man raised a toast to Danny and Elizabeth in turn, then took a long drink. A line of white sat along his upper lip. "Outstanding."

"Thank you. Trying to maintain the family legacy."

Elizabeth studied her competition. When Danny filled the next mug, a splash of beer escaped the rim. A rivulet dribbled over his fingers and down his wrist. He wiped the outside of the mug with the towel and then his hand. He traded that towel for a new one, then handed the clean mug to its owner. After each pour, he tallied whether it was a partial or full fill in a notepad. On the other half of the page, he had comments and notes for his next brew.

"Tell me more about this history of yours," Elizabeth said. "I'm told your long-lost relative is who we have to thank for this event. A brewer? Bet he or she never pictured something this big would materialize."

"Definitely not. He was a logger, my great-uncle. Another Sorenson. We're from a tiny town close to Denmark. He came over looking to build a new life in America."

Elizabeth gestured to the hollowed out pine stump on Danny's table. She smelled the richness of the wood. Beads of sap peppered the surface. "Is that where you get your inspiration?"

Danny nodded. He leaned his wrists on the rim of the stump. "I've even got a couple of his recipes. Or the notes, anyway. Had to use wild yeast back then, at least between supply runs."

"Makes sense." Elizabeth ran her hand across the bark of the pine. "Who wouldn't use what was readily available? Especially when you know it so well."

"Too well, I think. It was actually his hobby that killed him. Logging is dangerous as is. It was even more so back then. Double that if you don't come to work sober."

"The Dead Swede."

Elizabeth wished the words back into her mouth halfway through their exit.

Deirdre.

Danny's cousin was a possible murder victim. They were here, inside this theater, because of Danny's long-lost relative. If kicking oneself was possible without moving, Elizabeth would do it.

"So, you've heard the stories?"

If Danny was offended, he didn't sound like it. Elizabeth was grateful for the segue.

"Gary gave me a history lesson before the Tap Fest," she said. "An overview. Three graves. All loggers from the same mill. Big population of Swedish immigrants worked there. Now a...park, of sorts?"

Danny nodded. "Beautiful spot, but some swear it's haunted. Why anyone would want to camp there is beyond me."

According to Gary, The Dead Swede Campground in the Bighorns was reported to be near three graves. Historians agreed that one of those buried was a known logger who'd ended his own life with an axe. Gary explained that the first Daniel Sorenson was thought to be one of the two unknown occupants.

Danny untwisted the cap on his water bottle, poured some water into a guest's plastic mug. He swished the liquid around and poured it into a bucket at his feet. He filled the mug from the tap and returned it to the owner.

"The stout left in there would have buried my sour," he explained. To Elizabeth, he added, "I do miss the rinse stations we had outside. Looks like this keg is about done. I'll have to get another."

"Speaking of taps, I should head back to relieve Casey. Thank you for telling me about your family. We owe a lot of our modern methods to the innovations of those who didn't have as many bells and whistles for brewing but still made an amazing product. Save me a pint, will you? I'm dying to sample your beer."

"Only if you do the same. I sense a porch-side tasting session in our future. And, since you mentioned your brother..."

41

"**S**INGLE? COULDN'T BE MORE single if he tried."

Danny gave a quick nod and looked everywhere but at Elizabeth. "Thanks. Was, uh...asking for a friend."

Elizabeth fought to hide a smile. There was a shyness there. A risk taken.

While Danny chatted with the next few customers, she watched his interactions. Listened to him share a kind word with everyone. Asked a question about their mother, their crops, or how they were enjoying their day. She could get used to a person like this in their lives—Casey's life.

But hadn't his family member just died? Here, with him present. He seemed sad—or at least, thoughtful—sometimes. *We all wear grief differently. But still.*

It was then that she thought of Justin. Casey's past. Moving on. Time had a funny way of making heartache duller, however much it lingered.

When the next customer left with their mug, Elizabeth turned to Danny. "History there, with my brother. Tread lightly. He's half my family, and I'm a fierce and protective little sister."

"Noted. With full respect," Danny said. He shifted his jaw side to side, thinking. "What about you?"

"Me?"

Leia whined at Elizabeth's side. The dog sniffed at the air, then thudded her tail against the carpeted floor. Elizabeth reached down to stroke her flank. Buy a little more time. She liked talking with Danny. Wanted to know more about this man. His motives.

"I don't see a ring," he said. "I know that doesn't necessarily mean anything these days."

Elizabeth put a hand on her hip. "A third of people my age are single, thank you very much."

Danny held up his hands in emphatic surrender. "No judgment. Just curious."

Across the theater, Ryland pushed through the lobby curtains and headed their way.

The deputy was about her age, give or take a couple of years. He had a good job, was a nice guy. She'd yet to hear him talk of a wife or even a girlfriend, and the Wolfs hadn't mentioned one. Elizabeth wasn't the only one who was single around here. Or was she?

"Had a husband. Once," she said. "We had different ideas about commitment. Divorced. Moved here. Liked a guy. He died. Liked another guy. It got awkward. Liked another guy and he liked me back. Then he...didn't. I'm not single for a lack of interest." Elizabeth shrugged.

Danny rested his hand on hers for the briefest moment. "We risk a lot, sometimes. With our feelings."

Elizabeth leaned against the table. Thought about his comment. It didn't take long for her eyes to find Corbin and Hannah in the crowd. He had his arm around her waist. She leaned into him as they chatted with the Müllers.

Elizabeth shook her head. "I don't know if more is in the cards for me. Some days, I feel like I'll be crushed under the weight of my past decisions. Not sure I want to risk adding to that burden."

"I hear that. Today has only added to my record of bad decisions."

Elizabeth stared at the brewer. Before she could probe for details, Ryland joined them.

"Ms. Blau, Mr. Sorenson."

Danny's eyes went dark. Cerulean shifted toward twilight, the first showing of his serious side. "Deputy. Any news about my cousin?"

"Mr. Sorenson, I assure you we're making our way through the list. Down to our last twenty or so."

Elizabeth was one of those twenty. Casey, too. "Here for me? Or Leia?"

Ryland reached for the leash. "Have her back in a jiffy. Come on girl. Let's get you and me a break."

Leia was quick to her feet. Happy to lounge, she was even happier for action. Leia half-dragged Ryland to the exit, eager for exercise.

"Once a sled dog..." Elizabeth said. She waited for Ryland and Leia to move out of earshot. When they were gone, she added, "Ryland's a decent deputy. He'll find out what happened to Deirdre. See that justice is done."

Danny flipped the towel off his shoulder and wiped the table. "My cousin wasn't well liked. I know that. Heck, I couldn't stand her myself. But that doesn't mean..." His lip trembled, and he paused. Collected himself. "Sometimes family is all we have. Imperfect as it may be. Deirdre was a Sorenson—and someone wanted her dead."

42

E LIZABETH BRUSHED A STRAY tear from her cheek. With her next breath, she released a little of the pain she carried.

She thought of Rhett. Her brother. The absence of her father. A shell of a mother behind bars, several states away.

The people who'd become like family, here in Sheridan County.

In the richness of this realization, she mourned for Danny.

Casey interrupted. Threw an arm around her shoulder, oblivious. "Liz, I don't want to cut into social hour, but I sure could use a hand. See Chris over there?" He waved to a stout man in front of their table. The man waved back, a shy motion. "Promised him some of the manchego. Said he loves prickly pear anything. Wants to vote for us. Thing is, I need a chance to make more trays. As you can see by the line behind him, we're getting as popular as our new friend here."

Elizabeth gawked at the stream of people lining up for Blau. A few minutes of conversation gone by, and there'd been a stampede at her own table.

"That's the good news," Casey said.

"There's bad news?"

He pressed the fingers of one hand to his mouth and gave a series of quick nods.

"Out with it, Casey Blau."

"Tap's broke."

"What?"

Elizabeth took a longer look at their table. One jockey box was open, tubing yanked out. The other yawned open from the floor. Those in line kept looking toward Elizabeth and Casey, willing them to return with a solution.

"I tried to jimmy something between both of them, but it didn't work."

Elizabeth pressed the palm of her hand to her forehead.

"Don't worry, though. Big Ricky and I had an idea. He's on it right now. In the concession stand. We're trying to sort out the taps. Just have to find where they connect."

"I know." Both Blaus turned to Danny. He gave them a half smile, one dimple kicked into his left cheek. "I worked here one summer—as a kid. Most of us townies did at some point or another. I can show you...er, Big Ricky."

Elizabeth exhaled all the air in her lungs. "Alrighty then. Now that I've had a heart attack, show me. Please and thank you, Mr. Theater Usher. I can get us hooked up and running again. Maybe—probably."

43

A T THE FAR END of the lobby, a stack of event chairs pressed against a red velvet curtain. Stray kernels of popped corn collected dust. Torn tickets had escaped post-show collection, reminders of shows gone by.

Danny shoved fabric aside and pinned it behind the chairs. Its absence revealed a door. He tried the lock, but it held fast.

"Momentary delay," Danny said. He removed a Swiss Army knife from his pocket, a white cross stamped on the red, plastic body. He unfolded a thin blade.

"Invented in 1891. Soldiers called it Swiss because they couldn't say Offiziersmesser."

Danny wiggled the tool in a crevice and listened to the mechanics. "It is a mouthful."

With a tiny *click,* the knob gave way to the invasion.

Cold air brushed against Elizabeth's cheeks as she peered into the exposed space.

"Light switch is round here somewhere." Danny wrapped his hand around the door jamb and patted at the wall. A single bulb blinked on. He pressed the door open and held it for Elizabeth. With a deep bow and a sweep of his hand, he ushered her inside. "After you, my lady."

Stairs stretched down into the dim. Elizabeth grabbed hold of the railing and started her descent.

Each step brought cooler air to her forehead. The theater itself was warm. This place was a stark contrast.

Where the theater was toasty, full of talk and laughter, this space was dim and graying. Dank and quiet. Wooden steps made for sturdy footfalls. Near the bottom of the flight, a hallway led out from the landing.

Danny switched on his phone light and directed the tiny beam ahead of them.

"Basement?"

"Not big enough to be that useful," Danny said. "But I suppose that's what most would call it."

He lifted the phone so Elizabeth could see the space around them. Low ceilings, cobwebs, and dark corners. There was a room-sized nook in which several boxes were stacked, rolls of movie posters tossed on top. Danny walked what mirrored the length of the lobby. Elizabeth followed.

"Feels a little Phantom of the Opera to be down here," Elizabeth said. The subtle temperature drop sent goosebumps along her arms.

Danny kept walking. "Imagine being a sixteen-year-old running down here on your own. Got to where I was pretty fast at swapping out kegs."

"Since when is the legal age for serving sixteen?"

"No one was down here to see me do it."

They stopped when they reached the equipment. Custom-built containers housed a cooling system for the tapped kegs, the pump, and the lines to get the beer upstairs. The tubing threaded upward along the wall.

A second nook housed the untapped, pasteurized kegs and soda syrup boxes. A few chairs were scattered about. A thick dowel rested between two chair backs, a small saw on one of the seats. Dust covered every surface. The hallway ended at another door.

Danny pulled a thin, beaded metal chain that dangled from the ceiling. An incandescent bulb shed the subterranean area in a soft glow. "I'll check if any kegs are low. That'd be a quick switch after a line clean."

"I've cleaned more than one tap line in my day, you know. Happy to help."

"I've no doubt," he said. "Let me do a favor for a new friend."

While Danny hefted one keg and then another, Elizabeth studied the door at the far end of the room.

Different from the one at the head of the stairs, this one was made of wood. Flakey, muted green paint covered its surface. Blackness seeped in from underneath.

Elizabeth brushed her fingers across the knob, tempted.

"What's back here?"

44

DANNY KNOCKED AT A keg with his knuckles. A hollow *clang* echoed back. "Was always locked. Manager said it led to Xanadu, for anyone brave enough to make the journey."

"That a fact?"

"He was a lit major. Never checked myself. Too scared, I guess." He patted the lightest keg. "I'll get this line cleaned. Then we can get you hooked up. Chris won't get too mad, so long as I take care of the equipment."

"Chris?" Elizabeth poked at a backpack abandoned on a rickety chair. "These must be his?"

"Huh?" Danny followed her gaze. "Maybe. He's the theater owner. Left James in charge while he went hunting."

"Clipboard James?" Elizabeth grimaced. "He doesn't seem like the type who'd want his kegs swapped."

Danny headed for the stairs. "Leave James to me. I'll be back."

Footsteps faded up the steps.

With the brewer gone, Elizabeth returned her attention to the door.

Up close, she could see that it had once been blue, and before that, gray. Notches had been carved in short lines. Sets of five on the right side of the door. *Marking the days gone by?*

Elizabeth remembered a similar wooden landscape from childhood. She lifted a finger to trace one of the sets. One, two, three, four, five.

As a kid at her aunt and uncle's house, Elizabeth shared a room with two of her cousins. She'd been assigned the lower bunk. The upper bunk, occupied by a cousin who tossed and turned throughout the night, was a foot from Elizabeth's face. Sleep was scarce in that room. With a tiny pen knife no longer than her pinky, she'd carved fine lines to mark each night on the march to graduation.

She'd left home—that home—at the first opportunity. There'd been Christmas cards, an occasional barbecue. She never stayed long. What had happened to that bunk bed, those foggy, lost years, she didn't remember.

Elizabeth glanced up at the stairs and listened. Quiet.

Round and smooth, the knob made a neat half-turn in her hand. With a *click*, the mystery door opened.

Breath caught in Elizabeth's throat. With another glance to the stairs, she gave the door a light push. Silent and slow, the barrier gave way to space.

"Hello?" Elizabeth whispered the soft greeting toward the dark, half-expecting an answer.

There was none.

Tentative, she took a step toward the door. She pressed again against the wood. Swung the door farther on its hinges. A soft *thud* sounded when it met the wall.

Light from the bulb behind her eked a half circle in the distance beyond.

No point in being scared of a path that leads to paradise.

Elizabeth leaned in at the door frame.

Concrete flooring and block walls lined the tunnel. A smell of damp, mildew.

Where could it lead?

Two steps inside, she thought she heard the sound of an airplane engine above. A soft *flap flap* from somewhere ahead. She stood frozen, listening, until a breeze ruffled the stray hairs at her temple.

Spooked, she turned back, only to kick the toe of a boot into a pile of debris. Empty beer cans and crumpled paper rolled to the wall. She stumbled forward and yanked the door closed behind her.

Elizabeth panted, recovering from the fright. She backed away from the door and into the light.

Danny clattered down the steps. "Everything's all set. I told James not to worry, so of course that's exactly what he did. Can't help that. Which beer did you want to tap? Casey wasn't sure, so I said I'd ask before hauling a keg down here."

Elizabeth didn't answer. Her eyes were glued to the door. For the briefest moment, there'd been a flicker of light below the doorsill.

45

"YOU LOOK LIKE YOU'VE seen a ghost."

"It's nothing. I'm good." *Am I?* Elizabeth moved away from the kegs. Gave him space.

"Any chance you've got your beer key on you? Mine's upstairs."

Elizabeth dug for the tool in her back pocket. A double ended wrench, the tool had a hook for faucets, a bottle opener, and the ability to loosen and tighten hex nuts. "This one's lucky. Don't lose it."

"Is it now?"

"A man who taught me everything I know gave it to me. My mentor."

How many years has it been? Ten. A decade since she'd taken the job as a server at a Seattle brewery. When the owner saw Elizabeth spending all her breaks watching the brewing process, he took her under his wing. A week before he collapsed from a heart attack, he'd cheered her through her first solo brew.

"Must have been a standup guy." Danny swapped a keg of Blau brew in place of the empty domestic. He tightened connectors and tested the equipment.

"He was. A little moody, though. Didn't like his ideas questioned."

With a grunt, he tightened a connector. "Like Buzz?"

"The guy from the brewery?"

Danny checked the lines while he talked. "I've heard what my cousin did. What he accused her of doing. And, honestly?

I wouldn't put it past her. She once planted decoy Easter eggs so that the rest of us cousins would find empties while she hoarded the candy."

Elizabeth listened while he worked. Watched his hands move, quick and agile, over the equipment. Danny had the deft movements of confidence, someone used to solving problems with action. This was a man practiced in one of her favorite art forms.

"Maybe she did steal his recipes," he continued. "But he wasn't all sunshine and beaches as a boss—not at all. Kept his people all hours, claimed they had to get everything just right or he'd have to toss out the whole batch. Take it out of their pay."

"But he seems so...relaxed?"

Danny brushed off his hands on his jeans. "If I had retirement at the shoreline on tap, I'd be the epitome of relaxation, too. You're good to go. I already set your brother and Big Ricky on the task of moving your table over to the concession stand."

"Won't that give me an unfair advantage?"

"Only if you start handing out candy along with that cheese."

46

"WHAT'S WITH THE LAUNDRY cart?"

At the end of the lobby, there was a small, metal, wheeled cart surrounded by folding chairs. Crime scene tape connected the seat backs. Southern stood guard.

Elizabeth joined Casey at their new spot. Table, coolers, and chairs fronted the concession stand. Danny high-fived her brother before heading for his own station.

Rearranging their spread to flank the taps took a few minutes and some planning. The siblings were back in business. James hovered around the popcorn machine. He filled the hopper and flicked a switch. Light and heat. A minute later, pops sounded from within. The aroma of popped kernels filled the lobby.

"Dunno. Ryland was all over it with the twins, poking around. Had a long argument about none of them having an evidence bag. Called it in."

Rhythmic popping continued behind them. Warmth from the heater pressed against Elizabeth's back as she returned to filling mugs.

"James here says he'll keep the popcorn machine going. Help us stave off the starving."

"Shoot, this is fancy," a new patron said. He eyed the platters. After selecting a nibble, he lifted his mug to Elizabeth. "Thank you."

Plunk went the wooden chip in the bucket.

Popcorn joined the Blau offerings and word got out. Food helped. People flooded the lobby, more taster chips in hand.

Good cheer from the crowd was infectious, but Elizabeth was cautious. If there was one thing she knew from years serving alcohol, it was that even the happiest drunk wouldn't stay that way forever.

"Two, please," a voice slurred.

A pair of mugs slid Elizabeth's way. She looked up from the taps to meet the eyes of the owner.

Tristan waited for their return. His face sullen, bags under his eyes.

Elizabeth bit the inside of her lip and debated whether to serve him. "Released from your duties for the night?"

Tristan's chin nodded, a slow acknowledgement of her question.

"Makes sense, especially with us being stuck indoors and all. It's a shame. The beermobile is very cool."

"No, I'm done, done," Tristan said. Can't work for that man anymore."

Elizabeth thought of her conversation with Danny. His description of working for Buzz.

A heavy sob from Tristan brought Elizabeth's attention back to the younger man's face.

"She didn't deserve to die." Tristan's voice ached with pain. He set one mug onto the glass countertop and buried his head in his arms.

The concession stand had become Elizabeth's bar and she was its tender. She grabbed several napkins from the holder at her elbow and pressed them into Tristan's hand.

"No, she didn't." Elizabeth struggled for more to say. "I'm so sorry for your loss."

Tristan wiped at his face. The thin paper blotched with his tears. "I loved her. Once. I can't sit around and listen to people laugh and joke like we aren't all in here because someone died. Because Deirdre was murdered."

Elizabeth's chest tightened at his declaration. Guilt locked in her gut like a pit sunk deep in the peach.

Tristan ran his hands through his hair, then pushed back from the candy case. He wiped one hand down his face.

"Maybe you can check in with Ryland. See how close we are to getting out of here. I think we all could use a little distance."

"Somehow, I don't think I'll be able to shake this place. Mentally. Even when we leave. There are just some things you can't unsee." Tristan collected both of his mugs and plodded away, his eyes downcast.

Voices near the door stole Elizabeth's attention from the grieving man.

Southern left his post to meet a uniformed investigator at the door and give her an overview of the situation. Ryland walked the woman over to the laundry cart. He dragged two chairs out of her way.

The woman snapped gloves on and approached the bin. "Show me."

Elizabeth strained to hear more of the exchange. Too many people gathered in the lobby, curious and whispering. They blocked her view with their bodies.

Beside her, Casey sliced more cheese and used tongs to refill the trays. "You could just ask, you know."

"Huh?"

"I know you're itching to see what's going on over there."

Elizabeth sucked in her upper lip. "Okay, yeah. I'm curious."

"Go ahead. I've got it."

47

"WE HAVE TO TAKE it back to the lab before we'll know anything. You know the drill."

"Any chance you can rush this one?"

Elizabeth tucked in among those listening to the officers talk.

The investigator handed a sheet of paper to the deputy. "You and I both know how well that will go over. How about you buy me a pop for the road, and I'll see how persuasive I can be." She pointed at the refrigerated case behind Elizabeth. Shiny bottles of high-end soda lined each shelf.

Ryland ushered her to the counter. "Of course. What's your poison?"

"Root beer, if you've got it."

Both of the officers looked at Elizabeth, expectant.

She held her hands up in the air. "I'm only authorized to serve my own product. Something out of that fridge would be me stealing."

"Don't look at me," Casey added. "I was arrested for murder last year. Some would say that's a slippery slope to sarsaparilla theft."

"I got it, I got it," James said. He reached behind Elizabeth and Casey to select a bottle and handed it to the officer.

The woman attempted to twist off the cap but to no avail. She gave a little grunt, her face scrunched with effort.

"Hang on," Elizabeth said. "I've got a—" She felt the empty space in her pocket where her beer wrench should have been. "Casey, I'll be back."

"Again?"

"You were fine a minute ago!"

"I was hoping you could babysit the kids so I could go talk with Danny. You don't even like him, and you're the one getting all the airtime."

Elizabeth clamped her lips shut. Swallowed her retort. Casey was right. He'd given her ample time to explore while he'd been saddled with the beer, the snacks, and the dog for most of the event.

"Just one minute, I promise. I left something in the basement."

48

E LIZABETH PROPPED OPEN THE door to the lobby with a wooden wedge. She'd found the block next to the door-frame.

"All right girl," she said to Leia. "Quick as a wink."

Light switch flipped on, Elizabeth descended the stairs. The dog clambered down ahead of her.

There's no reason to be scared. Stairs are stairs. Darkness is only an absence of light.

People teased Elizabeth about her love of facts. Collecting them had started as a coping strategy. A means to drown out the sounds of family battles raging on long after bedtime.

One...two...three... She counted each step down the stairs, willing for there to be fewer than she remembered.

At the bottom, she was grateful for the continued burning of the single bulb overhead.

Leia sniffed at the recesses of the room. She moved in and out of shadows, on the hunt for a rodent plaything.

Her beer wrench was right where Danny had swapped the kegs. It rested atop the cooling unit. She'd been so distracted by her discovery of the tunnel she'd forgotten to grab it on her way out.

The cooling units hummed, a soft white noise in the dim space. Nothing had changed. The room looked as it had when she left it.

In five paces, she had the tool back in her hand. A twinge at the base of her neck forced her to look at the door. The one at the end of the room.

It wasn't latched.

The bolt extended out from the locking mechanism, pre-venting the door from fitting into the frame. *Did it close when I yanked on it—or popped open behind me? Or did someone else go through?*

Elizabeth dashed halfway up the stairs, unwilling to find out. She twisted back to call out, "Leia, come. Now!"

49

ELIZABETH AND LEIA BURST into the lobby. Elizabeth exhaled a big breath and steadied herself against a poster for *News of the World.*

At the front doors, Sheridan and Enid's voices lifted in a heated debate. Elizabeth ducked back behind her post at the concession stand. Casey nudged his chin toward the argument. This was their sign to eavesdrop. They continued handing Blau creations to the now-silent line of people in front of them. In small towns, no one wanted to miss a moment of potential gossip.

"I changed your diapers five nights a week so your mom could become a hygienist. Make a better life for you." Enid's curls shook with emphasis. The unruly halo was plastered back from her face with a paisley headband. Her eggplant sweater capped a pair of well-worn jeans and bedazzled cowboy boots. She held a large platter coated in sheets of plastic wrap. "I know she taught you never to look a gift horse in the mouth."

Enid was an institution on Main Street. As owner of one of the two coffee shops, Enid's business extended far beyond the town's favorite morning drinks. She had an ear for every story, a lap for every baby, and a cup of tea for every tragedy. Enid carried a personality so full of heart and vigor, she blew into a room like a spring storm, warm and nourishing. At the moment, she also carried a giant metal tray.

"We can't add people to the scene of a crime. You know that as well as I do. Have to keep it buttoned up. Secure." The officer had over a foot of height on the smaller woman. He looked down upon her small frame like a child.

"Point one, the crime took place out there." Here, she cocked her load onto one hip in order to point down the street. "Point two, you've had those folks locked up in there for hours, now. They deserve food. What good is it to be holed up with nothing but alcohol? Foolish. You should have called for catering hours ago."

"We've got popcorn," Sheridan spluttered. He turned and gestured at Elizabeth and Casey. "They've got hors d'oeuvres or whatever they're called."

Elizabeth waved at Enid. Enid waved back.

"I'll be back in two minutes," Enid said. "If you know what's good for you, you'll be waiting. Get a few hands ready to help."

Elizabeth mouthed, "Thank you." She'd sent Enid texts asking for backup. Enid had been happy to respond.

Enid winked over the officer's shoulder, shoved her tray in his arms, and left the way she came.

Bewildered, Sheridan set the tray on the concession stand. He peeled back the layers of wrap to reveal dozens of cookies. Sugar, oatmeal, cowboy, and others leaned against each other in a swirl of treats.

Casey snatched a lemon snap and shoved it, whole, in his mouth.

Elizabeth slapped at his hand. "Those are for the people inside!"

Casey chewed and swallowed. "I am a people inside. We've gone for hours on water and a slice of cheese. I'm fading away. No regrets. That cookie was fantastic."

Elizabeth eyed an earthquake cookie on the edge of the design. Sheridan selected a chocolate chip cookie. He gave her the slightest lift of his shoulders, as if to say, "You won't get an argument from me." He returned to his post at the door.

Elizabeth willed herself not to scarf everything on the platter. Casey made no promises, liberating a second cookie from the offerings.

Kachunk kachunk. Kachunk kachunk.

The sound of cart wheels preceded Enid's knock on the doors. Sheridan swung one wide open and then the other. Enid shoved her kitchen cart through the new opening.

"Don't worry, I'm not planning to come in. The last thing I have time for today is to get drawn into a murder investigation." Enid pointed to the containers on the tray. "I brought two pots of chili, and there's more coming. There's cheese, sour cream, and hot sauce. I loaded up every biscuit I had into that basket. I've also tucked a veggie quiche in there, hoping someone's got a knife to cut it up. You let me know when to pick up the tray, and I'll load it again."

Sheridan nodded. Elizabeth could smell the enticing aromas from her post. The officer had to be half-starved. Resisting Enid's cooking would take resolve most did not have.

"The correct response is 'thank you,' Ryan Mackey."

"Thanks, Enid."

"Now get this out to everyone before it gets cold. Better yet, find who killed that girl so we can all go home."

Sheridan—Officer Ryan Mackey—wheeled the cart near the concession stand. He set the cart brakes and lifted the biscuit basket from the bottom tray and added it to the offerings on the counter. Elizabeth shifted the various platters along to make room.

Casey lifted a lid and sniffed. "Heaven. Who's hungry?"

Those in the lobby formed a line, excitement peppering their talk. Beans & Biscuits not only served quality coffee, it was also known for its hearty, delicious fare. Enid's cooking was a community staple.

Elizabeth removed her apron. "I'll let everyone else know. Get a line organized so we don't have a stampede."

Word had leaked into the theater. Those closest to the door pressed out as Elizabeth pushed in.

"Let's just get the line coming down the aisle here, keep it from getting crowded. Enid at Beans has sponsored a treat for everyone. There's more coming, so no need to shove."

"I knew she'd figure out how to get it in," Gary said. Head barista for Beans, he knew his boss well. "I told her it was Mackey at the door. She said it wouldn't be a problem."

"She'd be hard to deny on a good day," Elizabeth said.

"Thanks for asking her over," Gary said. He patted Elizabeth on the shoulder and joined the line.

Elizabeth made her way to Danny's booth. She stepped around the line of drinkers to join him behind the table.

"There's chili in the lobby. Want me to get you a cup?"

Danny grinned at Elizabeth. "That would be phenomenal, thank you. I haven't had much outside breakfast."

Elizabeth didn't return his smile. Instead, she stared at an object tucked behind the hollowed out logs. She blinked several times, then her hand went to her pocket to confirm its contents.

On the table was a striped, beaded barrette. Black, red, and yellow.

50

"MS. BLAU," RYLAND SAID. "Your brother is next on my list. He's asked me to, and I quote, *'fetch* my sister.' He says you've had enough freedom for the both of you. Again, his words, not mine."

Elizabeth barely heard the deputy behind her. She pointed to the barrette and squinted at Danny. "Where'd you get that?"

Danny froze for a moment and studied her face. "Found it outside." His tone was evasive, and he angled his body away from Elizabeth. Busied himself with the contents of a cooler.

It was the first time he hadn't been open, ready with detail. His defenses were up, as were the fine hairs at the base of her neck.

What does Danny know?

"No," she said, her voice cold. "You didn't."

Slowly, Danny turned to face her. His jaw was set, his ears red. He leveled his gaze at her, emanating heat.

"Didn't what?" Ryland had reached the table. He waited, looking first at Elizabeth and then Danny while he waited for an explanation.

"That's not some random barrette you scooped off the street." Elizabeth's mind whirled with possibility. "Is that stuff in the basement yours, too? The backpack? Is that why you brushed it off?"

"What stuff?" Ryland volleyed his attention between the two speakers. He attempted to catch up.

"I've never seen that bag before. You were the one poking and prodding in places that aren't yours."

"Places? There's a basement? I'm going to need someone to show—"

"And I suppose you're going to tell me you didn't go back down there after I'd left." Elizabeth's heart raced. The accusations flew from her mouth, as though steered by a mind of their own. "You left the door open, you know. What's down there in those tunnels?"

Danny balled his hands into fists. Straightened to his full height. He took two big strides away from her, spun around, and stomped back. Elizabeth leaned away, one eye on his hands.

"I'm afraid of snakes. Okay? There. I said it."

Elizabeth's head flinched back. Ryland furrowed his brow. "What?" they asked in unison.

"She saved me, once. A long time ago. You know the old rhyme. Red and yellow, kill a fellow. Red and black, friend of Jack."

Deputy Ryland shook his head. "I haven't the slightest idea what you're talking about."

"Snakes," Elizabeth said. Her eyes were wide with recognition. "It's how you know which are venomous. You look at the stripes. If red and black are touching, like the scarlet king snake, you're fine. But if red and yellow are together, look out. You're in trouble."

"Coral snakes," Danny said, nodding.

"Thank you for the biology lesson, Ms. Blau. Unless you're about to tell me there's a snake loose in this theater—and I've definitely dealt with weirder things today—then I don't understand why we are talking about poisonous animals."

"Venomous," Danny said.

"Poisonous means you bite it. Venomous means it bites you," Elizabeth said.

Ryland huffed. He was a man rarely ruffled, but this conversation seemed to tax his patience. "Fine. Ven-om-ous. How did we go from a basement lair to snakes, and what does any of this have to do with anything of consequence?"

Elizabeth pointed to the barrette on the table and pulled its broken match from her pocket.

"How about you tell me," Elizabeth said to Danny, "why you have one of Deirdre's barrettes."

"Deirdre's?"

"One summer," Danny started, "we all went out east to watch her brother graduate from Marine boot camp. I wanted to see the fireflies. Didn't grow up with them out here. Must have been seven, then."

Elizabeth tried to picture a young Danny Sorenson. Before the growth spurts, before the shadow of a beard. Before the forehead lines began to crease.

"There was a snake in the grass. She saw it, dragged me away in time. Launched itself at her instead."

"Yikes," Ryland said. "That'd unnerve anyone."

"She was my hero. Taught me that rhyme and told me to stay away from snakes. Used my allowance to buy her those barrettes when we got home. I saw she was wearing them today. When I found one after...well. I didn't want to lose that piece of her I loved."

"I'm sorry," Elizabeth said. "I didn't know."

Ryland withdrew a plastic bag from his pocket and moved around the table. He used the bag like a plastic glove to scoop up the barrette without touching it. Ryland sealed the bag and patted its contents. "When the investigation is complete, assuming I get the all clear, you can have this back. Sorry I have to take it, but I think you understand."

"Better take this one, too," Elizabeth said, and held out the crushed pieces.

Ryland took out a second bag and Elizabeth tipped the remnants inside.

"Ms. Blau, Mr. Sorenson. You're going to need to come with me. I need to see this basement of yours."

51

THE BULB ABOVE THEIR heads flickered. Somewhere behind them, a rat or one of its rodent cousins scurried along a wall.

In the basement of the old theater for the third time that day, Elizabeth felt the walls press in upon her.

Ryland poked around the machines. He shone his flashlight into every crevasse.

Elizabeth stepped forward and pointed. "There's the backpack and the door to the tunnel and who knows what else. There was some trash behind it."

Ryland looked at Danny. "What am I missing?"

"There's not much to tell," Danny said. "This is where we stored stuff for the theater. It's been years, though. Not sure how Chris organizes things. Could be anyone's stuff." He shrugged and scuffed one foot across the concrete. "I never thought to try the door. Guess I believed it when I was told the passage was locked."

Hands on hips, Ryland surveyed the area. He unclipped the radio from his belt. With a button press, he called the others. "I'm going to be down in the basement for a few. I'll let you know if I find anything. Get someone to cover for Casey Blau so you can keep the questioning going. Ms. Blau will be up shortly."

Communication complete, Ryland traded the radio for his flashlight. He slipped on a pair of gloves and approached the backpack on the chair.

When he pulled on the bag's opening, a can fell out. It hit the ground and rolled across the floor.

Sounds hollow. She wouldn't risk picking it up, not when it could be evidence. Still. Curiosity clawed at her willpower.

Ryland gestured at the bag. "So, none of this is yours?" He peeled off first one glove and then the other.

Danny shook his head.

"Or yours?"

It was Elizabeth's turn to deny knowledge.

"Empty cans, an old bag. Could be something, I suppose. Likely nothing. How about you both show me where you found those barrettes."

52

RYLAND LED THE WAY across the lobby. Elizabeth and Danny trailed behind him.

Casey stared, open-mouthed. Elizabeth gave her brother a little wave.

"Unbelievable," he said, under his breath. "My sister gets to gallivant around with my crush, and I'm stuck here, serving her beer."

"Smarts, don't it?" said a silver-haired woman. "Now pour us some of that liquid gold. We aren't getting any younger, you know."

Elizabeth blinked at what was left of the sunshine. A few hours in the theater and her eyes had adjusted to dimmer lighting. Outside was brick and yellow, chrome and grass. Inside was red and gray, silver and velvet.

She hop-stepped to keep up with Ryland's long-legged strides. Danny matched the deputy's pace.

"I told you why I picked mine up. You didn't say anything about yours."

"About that," Elizabeth said. She was a little out of breath. A little ashamed. "I shouldn't have assumed."

Danny stepped over a fallen folding chair. "Water under the bridge. In a way, I kind of appreciate that about you."

"I all but accuse you of murder and you're cool with it?"

They were a few yards from the food trucks.

In their half circle, they took on the appearance of abandoned wagons along the Oregon Trail. Once full of hope and pioneers, now relics from the moment before history changed.

"You have the guts to stick to facts. Even when they might flush out ugliness. It's an uncommon form of bravery. Most would rather stick to what's comfortable. Routine."

This was an unexpected compliment. Elizabeth's cheeks flushed. "Most people find my recitations of facts kind of annoying."

"Most people are fools."

Elizabeth smiled at Danny. He returned the grin.

"If you two are done making friends, would you mind very much coming to show me where you found these items?" Impatience wrapped around Ryland's request.

"Found mine by the door," Elizabeth said.

"Which door?"

Elizabeth pointed back to the theater. "That one."

Ryland withdrew a permanent marker from his front pocket. He scribbled on the outside of the bag of broken pieces. "Okay, we'll go there next. Sorenson?"

Danny tapped a parking curb with the toe of his boot.

The molded concrete barrier sat behind the wheels of the mammoth beermobile. At its front end, wedges held each wheel for stability. Elizabeth pictured the catastrophe of a fully-loaded truck rolling down Main Street.

Ryland squatted to examine the spot below the tailgate of the truck. "On top here? Upright?"

"Yeah."

"Could have fallen out of her hair. Or someone else found it, set it up on the curb. We'll check for prints." He snapped a few pictures, then stood. He tugged on the back door of the truck.

"You have to kick it," Elizabeth said. She stepped forward, aimed for the corner of the door, and gave it a swift punt.

Ryland put his flashlight under his arm and tried the handle. The metal lever lifted, the door opened. With one hand on the side of the door and one foot on the threshold, he hoisted himself into the back of the vehicle.

The deputy crouched at the opening and shone the flashlight around the interior.

"What do you see?"

"Beer stuff. Coolers. Kegs. Tubes. Empty cans."

Crunch. Ryland's foot crushed one of the cans. The flashlight clicked off. Ryland extracted himself the way he'd entered, a spider-walk out of the cramped space.

"Not much room back there with all the beer," he said. "Always thought fire trucks had more room inside. They looked so big to a five-year-old me."

"Water tanks take up a lot of space," Elizabeth said. "Guessing they couldn't do anything about that in the retrofit."

Ryland scanned the parking lot where they stood. Empty of people, the distances seemed extensive. Clues could be anywhere. He turned on the heel of his semi-polished shoe, making a tight circle of observation. "What was she doing out here?"

"That's assuming she dropped it," Elizabeth said.

"Deputy—" Southern swung open the back theater door to the alley, just short of where Elizabeth had found Deirdre's barrette. "We need to get this crowd under control. It's getting wild in there!"

53

THEY RUSHED IN THE back door. Ryland pressed ahead into the lobby.

The space was empty. Elizabeth followed the others toward the crescendo of sound.

Music and rhythmic clapping welcomed them into the theater. Atop the stage was a foursome consisting of Big Ricky on guitar, Raj on the fiddle, and the Müllers. Otis played the banjo while Judy rattled a pair of wooden spoons across her knuckles and onto her lap.

People stomped to the beat as Raj broke into a rousing solo. He dragged the bow across the strings with such force and speed his arm was a blur. Big Ricky tapped his foot alongside. For the final measures, the other instruments ceased playing. All attention fell on the fiddle.

With his last stroke, Raj lifted his bow with a flourish. The crowd erupted in cheers. People rushed the stage, reached out to offer high-fives.

Big Ricky stepped to the mic. "Anyone have any requests?"

Folks pressed to the stage, shouting for reels, jigs, and Cajun tunes.

With a whisper and a nod to the band, Big Ricky counted the band in, and they were off on another song.

Joy flowed through the room like beer through the taps. People were happy, energized—and inebriated.

This will make for a rough morning for most of them, she thought.

Still, she was glad for the change in tides. If the night could end like this, she wouldn't feel too badly about a loss.

With a sudden urge to shake their box in an attempt to guess the vote count, Elizabeth searched the room for Casey. She should get back to the booth, collect any final votes she could get.

As if on cue, Leia nosed her side.

"Who's been watching you, girl?"

Leia had a can in her mouth. She shook it, gave a playful growl. At home, she loved to play tug with her squeaky toys and braided ropes.

"That's not a toy. You shouldn't play with those." Elizabeth reached to take the can. Leia pulled back. Elizabeth heard the crunch of her teeth on metal. "You're going to cut yourself. Drop it, Leia. Drop. It."

Reluctant, the dog set the can on the ground. Hung her head.

Elizabeth reached out to pet her dog. "Good girl. I'll find you another toy as soon as I can. Let me throw this one out."

She picked up the can. Counted the tooth punctures. Without any label, the exterior was otherwise a shiny, fresh aluminum. It was light. No liquid seeped through the holes. Either Leia had it long enough to drain or it was sealed while empty.

Elizabeth sniffed at the openings. *No scent. Then why seal it?* "That's odd." She shook the can. Contents rustled, soft against the canister. "Leia, what did you find?"

54

ELIZABETH HOOKED A FINGERTIP under the pull tab. With a *pop*, the metal top was punctured.

She held the can up to her right eye and closed the left.

Paper. There was paper inside the can. Elizabeth gave the can a firm shake and looked again.

Money.

Can in hand, she surveyed the scene around her, seeking a familiar uniform.

All attention was on the stage. The makeshift band burst into Orange Blossom Special. Feet tapped across the vast room. The sound design of the old theater meant amplification. Music filled the space. Stage lights shone on a sea of smiles.

Ryland watched, mid-aisle. He grasped opposite elbows and leaned over to confer with Mackey. The two looked over the crowd. Whispered.

Overhead, the moon of Southern's face appeared in the projection booth. He nodded in time to the music, the seriousness of his post on hold for the tune.

"Come on, girl." Elizabeth headed for the lobby. Leia followed.

The entryway was devoid of people. She crossed behind the concession stand and set the can on the floor. Leia approached.

"Wait," Elizabeth commanded. Leia sat.

Elizabeth lifted her foot and, with swiftness, crushed the can with her heel. She crouched to pick it up.

Leia cocked her head to one side, curious. She licked at her lips, impatient.

"No, you can't have it back."

Elizabeth held the folded rims of the can in opposite hands. She twisted the ends in opposite directions. The thin walls of the can tore along the crumpled ridges.

A wad of bills fluttered out onto the floor. Twenties.

She frowned at the pile by her feet. *Why would someone put money in a beer can?*

Elizabeth grabbed a broom and dustpan set from a nail on the wall behind the stand. She swept up the cash and the shredded aluminum pieces and dumped them into an abandoned jockey box. Replaced by the tap system, it had lain open, waiting. Elizabeth had propped it open to dry, an old habit from living in a damp climate.

Now, she kicked it shut. No one would think to check for cash in its plastic confines.

A knock on the counter startled Elizabeth, and she dropped the dustpan. It clattered to the ground. She snatched it back up and reconnected the pan to broom before hanging the set back on the wall.

Elizabeth took her time standing up. Half because she didn't like being summoned, half to give herself a chance to still her throbbing heart.

When she popped her head above the counter, she expected to see an impatient customer. Instead, Buzz leaned on the counter, sipping from a soda bottle.

"Interesting beverage choice, given the occasion."

Buzz regarded the bottle. "Gave up drinking."

"I don't understand." Elizabeth frowned. She rewound her interactions with the man. The idea of a master brewer who didn't drink was hard to reconcile.

"Got a little too attached to my product. If you know what I mean. Said and did things that cost me a wife. Then a girlfriend. Employees couldn't stand me. Couldn't stand myself and by then, my blood pressure was up." He sighed. "Something had to go, and I didn't want it to be me. These aren't exactly health food, but I have one when the urge to backslide into the dark days becomes too much. Just need to make it to that finish line, you know?"

"Your retirement," she said.

"Yeah." Buzz began to peel the label off the bottle.

Elizabeth remembered the earlier explosion. She wondered at the ache of watching your sweat, blood, and tears go up in smoke. The pain of not being able to do anything about it.

"How do you know when it's time to go?"

Buzz pressed his lips together, nodding. He turned his attention back to the brewery. "I'm looking forward to endless sunshine and miles of sand. But yeah, the passion has dulled a bit. A lack of a spark, no interest to innovate. I can't be on my game the same way, you know? If I don't actually care."

Elizabeth nodded. She regarded this person, about to move on from a business she'd give almost anything to have for her own. It was hard, in moments like this, to stuff envy down deep. Empathy had to win out, always. "How do you do it?"

"Do what?"

"Figure out if your beer is any good," Elizabeth said. "If you don't drink."

Buzz shoved his hands in his pockets, kicked at the carpet. "Hired someone to tell me."

"Tristan?"

Buzz nodded. "He isn't the first. But I trust him the most. I have to—and trust is hard to buy." Buzz gave a single shake of his jaw, his eyes lost in recollection. "It's hard to share your secrets. Talk details. Especially after being burned. I've said and done things I'm not proud of, all in the name of business. Wasn't supposed to be like this."

Elizabeth unpacked his words as fast as they spilled out. *What exactly did he say...and do?*

Buzz took another swig and continued. "So, I'm selling. Or trying to. I don't need much where I'm going, but I do need something. But now with this..." he gestured toward the wall between them and the damaged brewery. "Who knows when I'll be able to make that happen?"

"That's a lot of pressure. Sand between your toes is going to be one heck of a reward. I guess I'm surprised Tristan doesn't want the business."

Buzz shook his head. "The boy is too much of a fool. Lets his heart run away with his head. In business, sometimes you have to make cold, hard decisions. That's never been his strong suit."

Elizabeth reached into the cooler to extract another soda. She popped the top off the bottle and slid it over to Buzz. She'd shove some money in the till later. For now, she wanted to keep him talking.

"I'm too old for this," he said. "Tired. Trying to keep up with the industry is exhausting. Might have to close the place."

Sounds from the raucous lobby crowd leaked out from the curtains. "The community needs events like this, you know," Elizabeth said. "It's not the alcohol. I'm an outsider, and I can see what this does for them. It's a place for gathering. For good cheer."

"They need something. Not sure it involves me anymore."

Southern crossed the lobby to where they stood. "Mr. Gibson, would you come with me, please? Just a few questions. We're almost done with everyone."

Buzz let the door shut behind him. Before he left her, he tipped his hat to Elizabeth. "Good luck."

55

S OUTHERN PURSED HIS LIPS. He tapped his pen against the
heel of his shoe. A staccato rhythm against the sole.

Elizabeth leaned against the back of the chair and draped
her right arm over the back. She'd crossed her right leg over
the left. Her right foot bounced, anxious.

She'd known her turn in the hot seat was coming. Under-
stood and respected the necessity, even. Then Leia found the
can.

While she was stuck up there, the money waited in the
cooler, where absolutely anyone could find it. Casey, most
likely. Open the lid and pull out wads of money, no explanation. He would freak out.

Why hadn't Elizabeth told Southern the minute he came
for her? That would have made the most sense. You find
something suspicious, you tell the first figure of authority you
can locate. This is a lesson she taught to student after student
throughout the years.

Adults can help you best when you are truthful. Immediate.

So why am I waiting? Because she didn't like Southern. It
was harder to trust people you didn't like.

Leia heaved a sigh from her spot on the thin carpet. She'd
slumped against the wall next to her owner, rested her head
on her front paws. Elizabeth rubbed her tummy with one foot,
soothing. Even the dog was impatient.

"Ryland should be here any moment," Southern said. "Then
we can begin."

"Got any magazines while I wait?"

"She's funny and a brewer. What's not to like?"

"I've got a contest to win. Maybe Officer Mackey is available to supervise us so we can get going?"

Southern sucked in his cheeks, then puffed them out. Beaten.

The office was thick with quiet. A mishmash of furniture and history crammed in the equivalent of a broom closet.

Theater managers had to babysit film reels in case of snag, snap, or worse—fire. Books, receipts, and ordering took place in the tiny alcove while the performances played on the screen below. The switch to digital had simplified projection but had not eliminated the need for office space.

Minimal illumination from the desktop bank light cast eerie shadows on the officer's face. There was a slight hook in his nose, a cleft in his chin. Cut jaw, beady green eyes. Add his slicked-back, sandy brown hair and you had a face for the stage, all angles and energy. Southern sat in his chair like a wooden doll. Erect and bent, hands resting on his thighs.

His attention hadn't left Elizabeth while she took her time sizing him up. Instead, he waited, patient.

Perhaps this was a strategy. A means to getting the guilty to spill their guts. Silence makes people uncomfortable. Elizabeth was two minutes from spouting trivia to this uniformed buffoon.

"Taxpayer dollars are sure put to good use with us sitting in this room. Can't you record me or something? I've got a contest to win."

Southern glared. "You heard the mayor. The contest is canceled."

Elizabeth stood up. "Like heck it is."

"Please have a seat, Ms. Blau. Ryland will be here any minute and then we can—"

Elizabeth wouldn't sit. She'd been tolerant, calm. Then resourceful, dogged. She'd relocated and reconfigured an event for several hundred people. Made sure everyone had a good time. Was having a good time, right now. Did half the job for these peace officers who'd yet to thank her for that occupation.

"The contest is on. I restarted it. Me. I gave people something to do so they wouldn't lose it while you all bumble about."

Southern's face flushed. His hands slid down each thigh to squeeze his knees. "I'm sorry for the wait. I am." He inhaled, pushed the words through his teeth. "Your patience is appreciated."

Elizabeth, hands on her hips, tapped a foot in impatience. "Where are you from?"

"Excuse me?" Southern blinked, as though the seeds from a dandelion puff had been blown in his direction.

"I'm trying to be nice. Give you a chance to be decent. Make conversation to kill the time until I can get back downstairs," Elizabeth said. "I know you aren't a local. No one knows you. They won't trust you—like me when I got here. Still me, for some. This process of yours isn't going to turn up much. Nothing personal."

Southern regarded her, opened his mouth, then closed it again. He gawped like a khaki-colored goldfish.

"Casper? Cheyenne? Let me guess. Laramie?"

"Colorado."

Elizabeth paced the short distance from the desk to the filing cabinet. "Why here?"

"More questions," he said.

"Always."

Southern checked his watch, tapped his pen on his notepad. "I needed a change of scenery."

From up on the stage, the band finished a song. The crowd cheered, a thunderous sound that filled the eaves. Elizabeth poked her head outside the tiny room to listen. When the band picked up again, she turned back to Southern.

"Is that code for a breakup?"

"This conversation is supposed to be about you, not me."

Elizabeth crossed her arms. "How many years?"

Southern shook his head no, then stopped. "Just one."

Colorado. "What happened?"

Southern looked past Elizabeth and out the door. "Some of us are loyal people. Others...not so much."

"Then you've come to the right place," Elizabeth said. "You'll be hard pressed to find a more loyal county in the state. Before you know it, the memory will be long gone. Replaced by someone who won't step all over your heart."

"That how it worked for you?"

"Not yet," she said. *Not likely in my cards,* she thought.

From the threshold of the door, someone cleared their throat. Elizabeth and Southern turned to face the entry.

"Maybe rewind a half step," Ryland said as he entered the office. "I'm going to need someone to catch me up on how getting deep about our love lives will help us catch a murderer."

56

ELIZABETH OPENED THE LID to present the can. "So, that's how I ended up here talking about my ex-husband."

"I see," said Ryland, though his expression suggested anything but. He'd sent Southern to fetch the cooler and bring it to the tiny office.

"Sorry for the dog slobber," Elizabeth said. "It's the same with kids. You spend all kinds of money on the fanciest toy, and they only want to play with the cardboard box it came in."

Ryland peered into the cooler. Gave the contents a brief shake. With a gloved hand, he poked at them, as though they concealed a snake that could jump out at any moment.

"Sure is an unusual choice for a wallet," Southern said.

Elizabeth considered the officer with new eyes of understanding. What if what she thought was a cold, flippant demeanor was a front? A role he played. Someone he thought he needed to be for this town, his position.

She remembered those days after she'd taken Rhett and called the lawyer. While Elizabeth knew deep down it was the correct next step, that didn't make the reality of the afterward any easier. She'd become testy with anyone who questioned her choices. Sarcastic with those who asked if she'd thought things through.

Maybe Southern was another person who'd left something dysfunctional and was dealing with the fallout. Not an excuse for crummy treatment, but a reason. A call for empathy.

Funny, how much compassion came from a moment in someone else's shoes.

"Where did you say Leia found this can?"

"Not sure," Elizabeth said. "She was chewing on it. She's been with me the whole time unless she's been with you or Casey. She even went down with me to the—"

Basement. Elizabeth remembered going back down to collect her wrench. The cans among the pile of trash in the passageway. She'd accidentally kicked them in the dim light.

Perhaps they weren't empty, after all.

⸻

"Come with me," she said. "Bring the flashlights.

Elizabeth led the officers down the stairs and into the underground.

"I'd heard rumors," Ryland said. "Some folks talk about it. Haven't had to chase a case down here—yet."

"Some cities give tours of theirs. In Seattle, it's a whole experience."

"Guessing they have to figure out if it's all still safe," Ryland said.

"Safe?" Southern grimaced. "You don't think there are spiders or anything down here, do you?"

"Pretty sure spiders don't impact structural integrity. Arachnophobia aside."

"I was more concerned about the walls holding up," Ryland said. "In my experience, the older the facility, the less likely you'll find ninety-degree angles."

Elizabeth pressed on the wall nearest to her, feeling the stone for telltale history. If these rooms and passages were in frequent use, they could prove dangerous. *How many businesses still have access?*

The group approached the passage door. Elizabeth saw no light beneath, heard no sound from within.

"You can open the door," she said to Southern.

"Forced chivalry?"

Elizabeth held up her hands. "I don't have gloves on," she said. Southern blushed.

Ryland reached past them both to open the door. Flashlight at ear height, he scanned the passageway. At their feet, tucked near the hinges of the door, were a few scraps of crumpled paper. The cans were gone.

"I swear there were some here," Elizabeth said. They made a sound when I kicked them, I remember. There was some other stuff too."

"I believe you," Ryland said. He sent the beam down the floor of the corridor and up along the walls. "Something tells me we aren't the only people who've been down here today."

Southern unfolded one of the crumpled papers. He held up the sheet. The details were hard to make out among the crinkles, but Elizabeth saw a giant mug of beer and TAP FEST in large print.

"Guessing this helps us narrow the list."

57

RYLAND TURNED HIS FLASHLIGHT beam into the depths of the tunnel. Southern stepped closer with his own, to amplify the light. Elizabeth waited behind them. Past their shoulders was an unknown.

"I'm going to need to close this off," Ryland said into the emptiness. To Southern, he added, "I'll need to contact the folks for the city somehow. I need schematics, a map, a legend, or something to look at before I send anyone down there to check it out. I'm not risking personnel."

"Roger that. We have the mayor here, so it shouldn't be too hard to rouse someone who can find plans."

"You could also ask the business owners," Elizabeth said. "Unofficially, of course. Some of them are here, too."

"What do you mean?"

"That tunnel is headed north," she said. "We went from the west end of the building to the east end of the building down here. That means it could lead to any or all of the businesses on the other side of Brundage. There's the shoe store, the Elks Lodge...and the brewery."

"How do you know we're facing north?"

"Mental map," Elizabeth said. "Feel free to check me on a compass. I don't know about you, but when I head into an unknown place, I keep track of where I'm going."

Ryland hadn't taken his gaze from the tunnel. "We need to assume that while any person of interest may not be far, they also could have left the premises. Until we know where these tunnels go, and get a team down here to sweep for prints, I've got to assume they may be down here just as easily as they could be up there." He pointed toward the ceiling and the full theater above their heads.

The radio at Southern's hip erupted in static. Officer Mackey's voice came through on the channel.

"Text messages came through. Have them upstairs. Oh, and that woman from the coffee shop says she's bringing her ice cream machine. Said to tell you she's not taking your opinion on the matter."

Ryland waited, hands on hips. "Alright, lay it on me."

"Everyone gets roses. I'm after mushrooms," Mackey read.
"Mushrooms?"

"You know, toadstools. Morels and shiitake and the like."

"Who was that one for?"

"Didn't get sent. Was on the draft screen."

"What do you know about shiitakes?"

Elizabeth sat outside the manager's office door, awaiting the continuation of her screening. The trio huddled around a small tablet, her questioning forgotten. Elizabeth tried to make a plastic-covered chair comfortable.

To kill time, she read the movie posters. Images lined the hallway between the projection booth and the manager's office. Whomever had hung them had a preference for 1970s science-fiction and romantic comedies.

The back and forth from within the office was mind-numbing. She needed to remind them she was here and waiting.

"Shiitakes are loaded with B5, copper, and selenium," Elizabeth said to no one in particular. "There's a correlation for preventing prostate cancer, too."

Silence for two beats. Then, acknowledgement.

"Uh, that's...good?"

"Here's one from a Colorado number. I know that area code."

Elizabeth rolled her eyes. She was again relegated to wait.

"What's it say?"

"Asks when rent is coming."

"That ain't good."

Mackey spoke up. "She sent a message to another Colorado number, saying she would have something soon. That was this morning."

"Who owns the number?"

"Her employer in Colorado. She also sent a text to her roommate. Asked about the conifers in the Arapaho national forest. Wondered if they could go for a hike next week and check them out. Roommate gave us the code to unlock the phone."

"We can rule out self-harm if she was making plans for the future."

"Maybe," Ryland said. "But it's still early."

Elizabeth pictured Ryland inside the room. Chin propped on the tips of his fingers as he considered the evidence at hand. Ryland was not someone quick to decision. He made a slow and laborious work of almost everything in life. Whether cutting a ham steak or considering a crime, he would not be rushed.

"Then there is this last text," Mackey said. "She sent herself a whole bunch of numbers followed by some forest emojis. Plants and stuff."

Elizabeth's ears perked up.

"What numbers?"

"You don't want to know which emojis?"

"Fine, show me the whole thing."

The room was silent for a few moments. Elizabeth drew her heels up onto the edge of the chair. She wanted to leap off from the pressure of anticipation.

"Any idea what it means?"

"My mother-in-law is into sudoku. That's the extent of my experience with patterns and the like."

"We did a unit on that with our scout pack," said Southern. "I'll take a crack at it."

From in the hallway, Elizabeth itched to see the pattern herself. She loved all kinds of puzzles, especially those that required logic. Jo and Enid outranked her in jigsaws, but she could go toe-to-toe on others.

"Ms. Blau?" Ryland called to her from inside the office. "Would you care to come in here and take a look?"

Elizabeth was on her feet in seconds.

58

ELIZABETH STARED AT THE numbers, willing them to make sense in her mind.

Stoichiometry was one of her favorite units to teach in high school. This was because Elizabeth's own chemistry teacher, Ms. Monroe, was her role model. The woman made complicated science fun. They built molecules with Legos and wrote chemical equations for s'mores. Ms. Monroe made every student feel like a scientist.

Elizabeth echoed this in her own teaching. Kindergartners weren't ready for molecular formulas, but they had natural curiosity. Last week, she'd taught them food webs with gummy bears.

Today, she employed those science skills to check for patterns. Ryland allowed her a copy of the text and released her back to the concession stand. When Southern questioned regulation, the deputy replied that Elizabeth was the closest thing to a coding expert they had. Would he rather wade through a paperwork trail with Cheyenne?

Like the scribblings Ryland showed her earlier, there wasn't an obvious answer—yet. The B could mean boron, but PB could mean peanut butter before it meant lead. In chemical equations, specifics matter. Still, there had to be a pattern, and Elizabeth was on the case.

Elizabeth assumed the deputy had cleared sharing with his own boss, but that was not her problem now. She had a puzzle to solve.

Gary's voice interrupted her thoughts. "Thank you, folks. We're pausing the music for a brief moment. We want to express our sincere appreciation for our brewers and guests. You made it possible for us to continue the contest. Please check your pockets for any remaining ballot chips and cast your votes now for the best brew. Judges are coming around to collect the tubs so we can tally up for our winners. I've confirmed with Mayor Roberts that he expects us all to be released shortly so we want to be able to announce our winners. So—last call for votes!"

Elizabeth gave their bucket a shake. *It's full, but full enough to win?* Anxiety pressed against her sternum.

Better distract myself, she thought

Numbers in front of her, her gaze roamed the concession stand. If this were a classroom and she were one of her own students, Elizabeth would encourage herself to create a model. See where it balanced, see where it did not. Check for common elements. Threads.

Brightly colored boxes of candies lined the shelving underneath the glass countertop. The popcorn maker was silent but still held most of a batch. As their grandma would say, use what you've got.

After thumbing through the contents of her wallet, she slipped a ten dollar bill into the locked till. Then, she extracted a box of rainbow-colored gum drops from among the offerings. Using the metal scoop, she filled a small bag with popcorn—no buttery topping.

Elizabeth unfolded the paper again. She reread the sheet, then selected representations for different letters and numbers.

She'd covered the glass in a colorful spread of gumdrops when Danny approached the counter.

"Your brother around?"

"Said something about circulating to chat with his clients. I assumed he was in there with y'all."

"Must have missed him. I was hoping to start a conversation. See where that goes..."

Elizabeth gave him a half smile. "I'll definitely let him know you came by."

"What's all this?"

"Trying to figure something out. Using a strategy."

"Looks like a tasty one. What's the popcorn for?" He pointed at the bag.

"It's a snack now," she said. "Thought I'd need it. Turns out I have enough gumdrop colors."

Danny leaned against the glass countertop. "So what exactly am I looking at?"

"I've got the amounts and the order that something was written down. But I can't figure out what all the pieces mean."

"My head is already spinning," he said. "I'm having flashbacks to sophomore year."

Elizabeth chuckled. "It's not that bad. Take a look here. Since I have letters with numbers after them, I've chosen a different color of gumdrop for each letter."

"So far, so good."

"The tricky part is the letters themselves. I have F, H, O, and Y. These could all be elements."

"Fluorine, hydrogen, oxygen and...?"

"Yttrium."

"Yeah, that. But they have other letters in parentheses."

"Exactly. Only they don't make sense. Parentheses can be part of chemical equations, but not like this. Y(CAY) isn't a thing. At least not on this planet. This is what makes me think they stand for something else."

"Like an acronym?"

"Maybe—except see this one? It says 60M. The letter is after the number, not before."

"And it's in each set, the BT."

Elizabeth nodded. "Some of the letters make a pattern, but not all. This one is Y(SBT). They could be units of measurement, but not any I know."

"I know you teacher folk can read upside down and other such sorcery, but I can't." Danny came around to her side of the counter. He pointed at the sheet near her green gumdrops. "These seem familiar."

Deirdre's text messages included H(CAS), H(CIT), and H(MOS). Elizabeth had written them on receipt paper and set them above their associated pile of green candies. "How so?"

"Like maybe H, whatever it is—not hydrogen—has different variations," Danny said.

"Variations...variations...hmmm."

Varieties.

"Whoa. No way." Elizabeth picked up the paper again. Looked from it to the candy and back again. She smacked her hand against her forehead.

"What is it?"

"Citra. Cascade. Mosaic."

Danny gestured at the candy. "H is for hops!"

"Which means these could be—"

"Recipes? In that case..." Danny got quiet as he studied the configuration. "The BT has to be boil time."

"Yes! I'm thinking we have Fermentation and Yeast for F and Y. Maybe O is other, like coffee or grapefruit?"

Danny frowned at the gumdrops, then pulled out his phone. He scrolled with one finger and then quick-tapped it against the glass. "I can't believe her!"

"What am I looking at?" Elizabeth attempted to peek at his screen while he jabbed his pointer finger at the display.

"*My* recipe!"

Elizabeth's mouth fell open. Before she could respond, Gary's voice boomed over the sound system.

"All right folks, we are about to announce the winners!"

59

"PLEASE HAVE A SEAT, everyone."

Elizabeth could count on one hand the number of events in her life when time crawled, caught in a slow and aching warp. Walking down the aisle on the arm of her uncle. Waiting to be wheeled into a delivery room. Driving to her brother's house for the first time last fall. In each moment, fear and excitement duked it out in her guts. Unsettled and anxious, she could only wait out the pressure.

This moment would land on that list.

Danny offered his hand. Elizabeth shook his hand with her own.

"Best of luck," he said. "And thank you."

"For what?"

"I don't think I could have handled this. Today. Without a distraction. And new friends." He gave her shoulder a light touch before he moved off to find a seat.

Elizabeth claimed an aisle seat near the back, Leia on the carpet alongside. They settled in to wait.

Casey parked himself in the seat next to her. He rolled his shoulders back, crossed one ankle over the other. "We gave it our best shot. I dare say we were a triumph, no matter who wins. Seven catering jobs on the calendar. People want specialty flavors. All this despite issues with our taps, running out of ice, and a murder investigation on top of it all. You should be proud, sis."

Casey was right. Together, they'd made a name for themselves, overcome a stack of hurdles. Most important to Elizabeth, she'd chalked up a handful of new connections. Made a friend or two.

Then why do I still have a sinking feeling in my stomach?

Gary was at the microphone. "First, we'd like to hold a moment of silence in Deirdre Sorenson's memory."

Mayor Roberts mounted the steps behind Gary. The official whispered to an aide beside him.

"Thank you, everyone. We now want to thank our sponsors for this event. First, to the WYO Theater for hosting us in more ways than they'd planned. Also, our gratitude to Western Printing, Prairie Credit Union, and the F. O. E. A big thank you to our band—weren't they great?" Gary paused for applause. "Another huge thank you to Maximum Brewing for again giving our winning home brewer a tap in a partnership with potential, as we like to call it. Buzz Gibson, would you please stand?"

Buzz, seated near the stage, stood to receive the applause. He removed his hat and waved it to the audience. Cheers and whistles continued.

"We also had two last minute sponsors, each in their own way. We would not have been able to make today happen without either of their efforts. First, thank you to the best boss in the whole world for bringing us food. She's outside churning ice cream as we speak."

More cheers echoed around the room.

"Last but not least, we owe one of our newest competitors our gratitude for getting us up and running after today's tragic events. Please raise your glass to Elizabeth Blau."

Casey let out a whoop and leapt to his feet. He was joined, row by row, by the entire audience.

Applause drowned out the doubt in Elizabeth's mind. A tear fell across her cheek.

"Thank you, everyone," Gary said. "Now I'd like to turn this over to our mayor to announce our winners."

Elizabeth gripped the arm rests of her seat. Her nails dug into the padded fabric. Casey leaned forward, elbows to knees, to rest his chin on steepled fingers.

"Hello again, everyone," said Mayor Roberts behind the microphone. He cleared his throat. "You've been patient and understanding. Thank you so much for cooperating with law enforcement. It won't be much longer. Gary and I have tried to do our best justice to all the entries. We appreciate our entrants for putting forth an amazing selection. Without further ado—James, do you have the envelopes?"

James handed up two red envelopes from below the stage. Roberts reached for them. He glanced at the writing on the top envelope before returning to the mike.

"Tonight the Sheridan County Historical Society is presenting a special award. This award recognizes outstanding contributions to our county's history." The mayor tucked his thumb under the seal and pulled at the paper. He removed the card and read its front. "Sheridan County wishes to recognize Daniel Sorenson for his work to preserve our history. His recreation of vintage brewing methods made for a showstopper beverage if I do say so myself. He has earned the first Sheridan County Heritage Award."

Danny took to the stage to shake Roberts's hand and smile for photographs. The mayor waited for him to return to his seat before he continued.

"And for tonight's top award, the People's Choice for Best Brew."

Elizabeth's mouth was dry. She swallowed. Her reflexes whined, ached to run. She wanted to dash for the lobby. Escape for some water. Some air. Anything other than subject herself to scrutiny. To failure.

"In a typical year, we tally your votes for half the weight and then add in our own. For our tenth anniversary, and moving forward, we want everyone's votes to count the same."

Casey leaned over to whisper. "You've got this.

Elizabeth held her breath, squeezed the arms of the seat until her knuckles went white.

Roberts tore into the second envelope. He blinked once at its contents. Recovered, he read from the card.

"This year's top brewer is Elizabeth Blau for her Rosehip Sour."

Elizabeth's heart skipped a beat. Her mouth open, eyes wide, she looked at her brother in disbelief. Casey reached for the end of the leash. Elizabeth stood, numb. While she'd wanted—*needed*—to win, she'd thought the prize would go to Danny. Blau Brewing had put up a good fight, but she'd seen the lines in front of his booth. Mug after mug. That she'd won the vote didn't seem real.

"That's impossible!"

60

ROBERTS LOOKED TO GARY and then at James. Gary took the card from the mayor's hand. He read one side, flipped it over, and checked the back. James wrung his hands.

Tristan rose from his seat. He put both hands on the seatback in front of him. "I said, that's impossible. I demand a recount!"

Before he could utter another word, Ryland and Mackey clapped hands on his shoulders. Shoved him back down into the chair.

"Tristan Gibson, you are being charged with the murder of Deirdre Sorenson. You have the right to remain silent..."

Elizabeth and the crowd gasped. They watched Officer Mackey remove a pair of handcuffs from his belt. He wrestled Tristan to his feet to slap on the metal bracelets.

"What? You have the wrong guy!"

The officers dragged Tristan toward the aisle. He struggled to get his footing on the way to the lobby.

Gasps and whispers were all that punctuated the otherwise silent theater. All watched as the brewer's assistant struggled against the constraints.

"I didn't kill her. I swear! She was already dead. You all saw her like I saw her. You have the wrong guy. Honest!"

"Right, buddy," Southern said. "I'm sure you didn't try to rig the judging either."

"Okay that was me, but it didn't work. She still won. That should count for something, right? That doesn't mean I murdered Deirdre."

Elizabeth slunk down in her seat as the group approached their row. *Did I win in a legitimate contest or not? Did Tristan kill Deirdre, a woman he said he loved?* She swallowed her shame.

"That's for a court of law to decide."

Ryland interrupted their exchange. "We've read you your rights. Both of you need to keep those rights in mind until we can get to the courthouse."

"You've got to believe me. I didn't kill her!"

The officers dragged him toward the door. From several aisles back, Mackey called, "I've got his bag." He had the crook of a gloved finger in the top loop of a familiar black backpack. A red and yellow ribbon was tied to the front zipper. It fluttered against the canvas.

Before the group could press into the lobby, Tristan shoulder-checked Southern. When the officer stumbled, Tristan made a run for it, cuffs and all. Ryland tackled him to the ground.

Mackey ran up the aisle to help subdue Tristan. When he passed Elizabeth, a can fell out of the half-open pack and rolled to Leia's front paws. The dog snatched up the new toy with glee.

"Wait!" Elizabeth stooped to retrieve the can from a reluctant Leia. She called out again. "Stop! I believe him!"

61

"**S**EE, I'M INNOCENT!"

Ryland pulled Tristan to his feet. Officer Mackey assisted.

"I don't know about innocent, but he didn't kill Deirdre. He also wasn't stealing recipes. She was."

"Ms. Blau, please wait here. Also, consider waiting to make any further statements until my return." Ryland and the other officers escorted Tristan from the theater.

Attendees got up from their seats. Regrouped. Some to congratulate Danny, others to stretch, but at heart, to gossip. All were curious, none were silent.

Elizabeth stayed put.

Casey looked at her, then back to the stage. "So...is there something you want to tell me?"

"Better not. Keep your hands cleaner that way."

Casey sat back in his seat. "You have my number if you need me to bail you out."

Buzz approached, hands in his pockets. "Brewer and crime fighter? That's quite a resume."

"Don't forget teacher," Casey said.

"Lucky kids. I owe you a thank you. Mind telling me how you know what my former employee was up to?"

"Deirdre or Tristan?"

Buzz sighed. "Both."

Ryland returned, Sheriff Wolf alongside him. The sheriff spoke into the radio clipped at his shoulder, then addressed them.

"I'll do the asking for a bit, thank you, Mr. Gibson," Wolf said.

The sheriff was a broad-shouldered man with a gruff voice and mustache to match. Elizabeth saw Wolf, her neighbor outside his job. Knew the man who built fences, read Chaucer, and adored his wife, Jo. Last Sunday, they'd played a rousing game of blackjack in which the sheriff bet his barn duties for the week. He lost to Jo's royal flush. While Clint mucked the stalls, Jo and Elizabeth shared a bottle of wine and teased him.

All jokes were behind them now.

Wolf tipped his chin toward Elizabeth. "Ms. Blau, can we ask you a few questions about your recent statements? Perhaps somewhere with fewer distractions."

"I have a quick question, first." She turned to Buzz. "Does Maximum Brewing have a crowler machine?"

Wolf raised an eyebrow. "I don't see what this has to do with—"

"We do. We're the only ones who have one at the moment. The new brewery up the street has one on backorder. They can be hard to come by out here, and they sure ain't cheap."

Ryland asked, "What's a crowler machine?"

"It's a machine that seals the cans of beer," Elizabeth said. "That way, customers can take home cans of what's on tap."

Ryland scratched at his temple. "Couldn't you use a hammer or something to tap or squeeze the lid on?"

Buzz scoffed. "Not if you care about your product. All you'd do is mangle an aluminum can. You'd have to do it over again. Crowlers help you ensure that the product lasts longer, too. Carbonation is important. Some of them are good for a couple days—if done right."

"Why did you ask?" Wolf set his brows in a line and waited. In his hands was a clear bag with the found can inside.

Elizabeth pointed at the evidence in his hand. "Because if I'm right—and I'd bet a month of barn duty I am—that can will contain a roll of twenties."

Ryland smacked a hand to his forehead. "The prize money."

Tiny rooms become more crammed with added bodies. Wolf ensconced himself, Ryland, Elizabeth, Buzz, and Danny into the tiny theater office.

"Tell me about the tunnels."

Danny took over. "I don't actually know where they go," he said. "It was always sort of a legend when I worked here."

"This one heads north," Elizabeth said, pointing.

"Is there a chance one reaches into the brewery?"

Buzz shook his head. "Used to. It's been sealed. Had to for insurance purposes, about six months ago."

Ryland held his chin in one hand. "Sealed in one location doesn't mean it's that way everywhere."

Elizabeth wedged herself into a corner of the office to think. Ryland straddled the manager's chair, the seatback to his chest. Wolf blocked the doorway with his bulk.

"You think," Wolf said to Elizabeth, "that Tristan sealed the money into cans?"

"And why the explosion?" Danny crossed his arms and leaned against a wall. "Was that some kind of diversion so he could get back over here without being noticed?"

"We don't know what happened at the brewery, yet. If something happens to a system, you have alcohol in abundance—all it would take is a spark. Even if it was Tristan, it could have been an accident."

"This is a dangerous game for my son to play for a few thousand dollars and an ex-girlfriend," Buzz said. "Besides, the crowler machine is in the beermobile. He wouldn't have needed the underground."

"That fire truck?"

"Hang on," Elizabeth said. "He might have been after something else."

62

ELIZABETH SUMMARIZED THE HEATED exchange she'd overheard.

"She wanted him to steal more recipes," Ryland said.

Sheriff Wolf had his notebook out. He scribbled across the pad of paper. "Sounds like we need to look into an earlier situation involving intellectual property."

"We've all heard the rumors, Sheriff," Ryland said. He hung his head. "Even family."

"Don't know about the past, but she definitely had some today." Elizabeth explained the pattern she and Danny had cracked. *Was it really just this afternoon?*

Danny closed his eyes and leaned his head against the wall. Elizabeth thought how hard it must be to hear his cousin's actions laid bare.

"What doesn't add up is that he told her no. He wouldn't do it," Elizabeth said. She replayed the argument in her head.

"Mr. Gibson, once we get the all clear, we can verify whether your intellectual property is still on the premises."

"There's a chance he'll confess," Ryland said. "That will streamline things a bit."

"...find yourself a new golden goose—that's it!"

The four men looked at Elizabeth. She had her eye on a paperweight on the manager's desk. A faux Oscar statue anchored a stack of invoices.

"Ryland," Elizabeth said. "Can we take a look at those voting chips?"

"Most winners don't ask for a recount," Ryland said. "But I'll fetch them." He left the cramped room.

Sheriff Wolf tucked his pencil behind his ear and looked down the length of his nose at the notes. He held the pad closer and then farther away, seeking his reading distance.

"No glasses today?"

"Don't tell Jo," Wolf said. "Forgot them on the roof of my patrol car. Just like she said I would. Likely a crunched pile of glass and metal at this point."

Danny snagged a pen from the desk. He chewed on the cap, ruminating. "But If Tristan said no, then why—and how— did he end up with the prize money?"

"Maybe for love," Buzz said. "Maybe to get back at me. She must have paid him with the prize money. I wasn't exactly a fan of their relationship."

"Possible," Elizabeth said. "Still points to his innocence. She was the one who would be using the recipes. He had cash—nothing on paper. Why kill her?"

"Here we go," Ryland called.

Wolf moved to allow him entrance. Ryland set the bucket full of wooden discs on the desk. Elizabeth upturned its contents onto the surface.

"Prove I lost. Not the game I thought I'd play," said Danny.

"Help me look," Elizabeth said. "Make stacks of ten. We are looking for any that look different. Close, but not quite the same."

Danny and Ryland helped her paw through the pile. They'd flip over a token, hold it up in comparison to the next. Separate it into a pile. Repeat.

Elizabeth began to lose hope. Stack after stack of the same wooden chips.

Just then, her fingers closed around a piece with rougher edges than the rest.

When held at arm's length, it was the same size. Up close, and when paired with others, the difference was clear. "We're looking for more like this," Elizabeth said, holding up the chip.

"You're right," Ryland said. "It's a completely different color."

"Projection screen paint," Elizabeth said. "There were cans of it in the basement. If there's one thing I've learned from my brother's design business, it's that one black does not equal another black. Paint matching is serious business."

Within minutes, they'd separated several dozen false tokens from the pile on the desk.

"I knew it," Elizabeth said. "He rigged the votes." The weight of her words fell to her feet. That meant that her victory was anything but. She shrank back from the gut punch of emotion.

Triumph gone sour like her rosehip brew.

"That dowel in the basement. He sliced them off, made his own." Danny looked at Elizabeth. "But why?"

"Wait a minute," Elizabeth said. She did a quick count on her fingers. "Where's the sixth can?"

63

"I T MIGHT NOT BE a six-pack," Danny said.

"But what if it is?"

Officer Mackey interrupted their conference.

"Enid is back. Brought a big bucket of ice cream. Says don't you dare let it melt before she can dish it out to everyone. She said I'm on sprinkle duty."

Sheriff Wolf pressed his lips together. "We need to get everyone packed up and out of here."

"But we still don't know what happened," Danny said.

"We can't hold a few hundred people hostage in the meanwhile. The investigation could take weeks—if we're lucky. We do have leads, we'll have his fingerprints, and we'll get there."

Danny, sullen, stared at a spot on the floor.

Wolf addressed the officers. "Let's release folks in stages. Guests first. Then the brewers and volunteers. Then we will do another sweep of the place. You have the list of attendees, participants, and volunteers?"

"We do. Notes and everything. Ms. Blau was our last person," Mackey said.

"Bring the notes to the station, and we'll cross reference them when we call people back." Wolf turned to Ryland. "Check people off as you release them. No mad dashes allowed. Verify contact information, especially for anyone who isn't local. Get license pictures. They're all adults. Mayor Roberts and Mr. Price can help with crowd control. Make announcements, give directions."

Upon Elizabeth's dismissal, she was hit with a wave of exhaustion. Between the murder and competition, the socializing and strategizing, she ached with fatigue. She wanted a hug from her son, a warm bath, and an early bedtime—in that order. She was wrung out, like a dishrag after a dinner party.

"I don't know about y'all," Gary said. "But ice cream is a must after this day."

Ryland addressed those in the lobby. "Everyone will be released shortly. Stay where you are until called to leave. I repeat, please stay in place until we can check you off. We will be releasing you in groups. In the meantime, Enid brought ice cream for everyone to enjoy."

"If I can stay awake long enough to pop a spoon in my mouth, I'm in."

"Any chance of chocolate?"

"I've had more than enough beer for two lifetimes. I need to get home."

In the lobby, a line streamed inward from the front doors. Mackey joined Enid behind her cart. The woman scooped great mounds of the cold dessert into cups she then passed to Mackey. He topped each with whipped cream, chocolate sprinkles, and a cherry.

"Don't be shy," Enid said to the crowd. She scraped at the side of the canister. "Step on up."

"Looks delicious," Elizabeth said. She'd joined the line. If brewers had time to wait, she might as well enjoy some ice cream.

"It's called Family Movie Night. Popcorn and candy pieces swirled into the vanilla."

Elizabeth stood to the side of the doorway and dug into her treat. The sweet crunch of the candy was balanced by the salty popcorn. "It's delicious."

"How is the investigation going?"

"Not fast enough," replied Elizabeth. She licked the spoon to savor the last bite. "This helps."

Elizabeth watched her friend dish out scoop after scoop. The ice cream was solid but still soft. Enid dipped her arm into the metal container and scraped at the bottom of the canister. "Almost empty."

Those at the front of the line groaned.

"Never fear," Enid said. "Give me five minutes and I'll have another batch."

"Can I help?"

"For sure. Add the contents of that pitcher into this container."

Elizabeth steadied her hand as she poured a stream of creamy contents into the container. She could smell the vanilla, black flecks against the white.

"You can set that bowl of candy and popcorn next to me. I'll stir them in after you add the dry ice—so the popcorn doesn't have time to get soggy," Enid explained.

"Dry ice?" Elizabeth set the bowl next to Enid.

Enid continued her instruction. She gestured with the ice cream scoop. "Reach in there and take out the dry ice."

Elizabeth opened the box to reveal a hunk of dry ice in a plastic bag.

"We could have used this earlier."

"Gary said the brewers had loads left over. Nothing like it for a fast freeze. Take it over to the counter and give it a bunch of whacks with the side of the meat tenderizer. We're looking for super small bits."

Elizabeth pitched an eyebrow. "What kind of Halloween prop is this?"

"You wanted to be helpful."

"Fine." Elizabeth walked the bag over to the counter and bashed it with the metal mallet. Five whacks shattered the contents into tiny pieces.

Enid pushed the now empty bowl her way. "Go ahead and sprinkle a few spoonfuls into the bowl. Quick now."

Elizabeth followed the guidance. Enid churned the ingredients. Within seconds, the mixture thickened.

"I need to do this with Rhett. He'd love it," Elizabeth said.

"The science or the ice cream?"

"He's my son, so, both."

Elizabeth tucked the tools back onto Enid's cart. When she reached for the remaining ice, she stopped. A fine mist floated off the chunks and toward the floor.

The Müllers received their sundaes. They gushed over the flavor to Officer Mackey. "I'm the sprinkles guy. Enid is the mastermind behind the ice cream."

"Yoo-hoo. You all right over there?"

"I'll never tire of watching sublimation. It's so cool."

Enid plopped a hunk of ice cream into another cup. "Sub-li-what?"

"Sublimation," Elizabeth said. She continued to watch the faint swirls of vapor. "It's when a solid skips straight over the liquid form and becomes a gas."

The line eased, and Mackey wiped at his forehead with one arm. He looked over at the dry ice. "I thought gas floated."

"Carbon dioxide is denser—and colder—than air. So, it sinks."

They all watched the transformation, mesmerized. Tendrils of vapor twirled and tumbled off the cart.

Elizabeth pressed her fingers to her lips. "Enid, where did you say you got the dry ice?"

"From the coolers." Enid pointed at the one on the lower shelf of her cart. "Turns out a beer fest is full of the stuff. Best way to super chill beer, according to Gary. Works wonders for instant ice cream, too."

Elizabeth froze as a chill zipped down her spine. It wasn't the ice cream. She took her empty cup and made a beeline for her brother.

Casey licked at his own dish, unwilling to miss a sprinkle. Elizabeth leaned in and whispered in his ear, "I need your help. Outside. Now."

64

C ASEY FLATTENED HIMSELF AGAINST the back wall of the theater. "I would prefer to remain here, thank you very much. Then I couldn't be charged for fleeing the scene of a crime."

"This isn't the scene of any crime," Elizabeth whispered from her own perch near an emergency exit. She'd slunk, cat-like, to the door. "We're going to the scene. Or near it, anyway."

Her brother rolled his eyes in an exaggerated arch. "Oh good. Now I feel so much better about this ridiculous plan."

"Sarcasm isn't helpful."

Casey continued to watch over his shoulder as he edged toward the door. "Wolf is going to kill us."

"He won't kill us if we get back before anyone notices."

Elizabeth pressed the bar to the door. The metal made a soft *ka-chunk*. She winced. A sticker slapped across the backside of the door alerted them to a likely alarm. Instead, as predicted by Danny, there was silence. She pushed the door open, the resulting crack bringing fresh air and city sounds.

Elizabeth checked that the indoor revelers were still distracted by ice cream and impending freedom. She whispered to Casey, "Come on. Let's go." She snaked first her hand through the crack, then an arm, her shoulder, and the rest of her body. She found herself in the alley, its sole occupant.

Casey slipped out the door behind his sister. "What now?"

Without a word, she beckoned to him to follow her.

The Blau siblings squatted low for their approach. They gave portable toilets a wide berth as they hustled by, ducked down with knees bent, arms spread for balance.

Their pace slowed as they neared the back of the beermobile.

Still open, the shiny metal glinted in the sunlight. Its inaugural run marred by the death of its honorary passenger, the vehicle was as ominous as it was bright.

Elizabeth twisted her head to check for witnesses to their intrusion. The area was empty. Only a tail of yellow crime scene tape flipped and twisted in the breeze. One end was tied to the stage, a remnant.

In front of them, the beermobile was silent. The row of taps gleamed. Two mugs waited for a fill, the passenger window rolled down.

'Hop in," Elizabeth said. "I'll cover you."

"This is your idea. Why aren't you going in?"

The twosome stood in front of the open back door, a stand-off.

"I'm more convincing when I lie," Elizabeth said. "Remember the laundry room window? The gummy bear incident?"

A deepening shade of scarlet flushed along Casey's jaw to his hairline.

Since he was a kid, her brother's ears were a dead giveaway when he lied. Whether he'd thrown a ball through a window, failed a test, or trampled his father's prize tulips, he'd been unable to deny his involvement due to the bright red evidence to the contrary.

Elizabeth, however, could lie like a champion, fooling everyone—even herself. When Casey snuck out one night to drink with his friends, he'd spent most of the next morning in the bathroom over the toilet. Elizabeth told their parents she'd dared him to eat an entire bag of gummy bears. No one doubted her.

"Liz." Casey grabbed the sleeve of her shirt. "What if you're wrong?"

"Then we sneak back inside. No one knows any better."

Casey pulled work gloves from the back pocket of his jeans and slid one on each hand. He put a knee on the bumper, took hold of the opening, and hauled himself inside with a grunt. "Next time I decide to rodeo my twenties away, remind me I'm a fool."

"You wouldn't have listened."

Casey crouched in the opening. "You aren't wrong."

Elizabeth reached up to grab the handle of the rolling door. She gave a gentle tug, and the door came downward. She left a gap at the bottom. "Can you hear me? Can you see all right?"

"Yep," he said. "It's dim, but I can see. Now what am I looking for? It's bigger than you'd think in here."

Elizabeth stood with her back to the vehicle, watching the theater. Ryland must have begun to release the crowd. A steady trickle of people exited the doors of the theater. From her post, she watched them blink at the streetlights and filter outward to their cars. The food trucks and tents were cordoned off, but when they began to release the brewers, that status could change. What was a reconnaissance mission could look a lot like a cover-up to anyone else. They had to hurry.

"See if anything is out of place. Like someone was messing around with something."

Shuffles and scrapes were heard from within. Another handful of people left the theater, some headed north, some south.

"There are a bunch of tubes. Kegs, of course. In some kind of custom freezer. Stack of coolers outside it. A few are open, but empty."

More people left the WYO. When a couple peeled off to head for the booths, Elizabeth's heart thudded against her chest. The Müller's were steps from their booth—and a direct line of sight to the beermobile.

"Casey, hurry. Please. And don't touch anything!"

Judy removed their tablecloth and folded it over one arm. Otis removed their flag from the front, tucked it into a large tote bag.

More shuffling from inside the beermobile. Sliding. "Huh."

Elizabeth whispered from the side of her mouth. "What is it? What do you see?" Her pulse whooshed in her ears. Every muscle tensed, like a horse at the race gate.

"The tubing is a jumble. Like someone disconnected a few, got them mixed up. Knotted. Here's someone's lunch box. No lunch, though."

Elizabeth heard another slide.

"Bingo!"

"Shhhh!" Elizabeth waited two beats, her eyes on the older couple as they bustled about their booth. Neither looked her way. "What is it?"

"Behind the lunchbox. Cylinder. About five inches long, A couple inches in diameter. No label."

Elizabeth grinned. "Bingo, indeed. Whatever you do, don't touch it. I bet her fingerprints are all over it."

"Proving what, exactly?"

"That she was the one trying to steal the recipes. Not Tristan."

"Okay, Sherlock. Now get me out of here. It's creepy."

Elizabeth glanced back at the theater doors. The firemen had been released to join the others in cleanup. "Come close. I'm going to keep it low. Folks are starting to come this way."

She heard Casey's steps along the metal floor. A pause, then his voice again, closer. "Ew. Ugh, oh this is gross. Do you have your phone?"

Elizabeth stuffed her device in the gap under the door. "Let me wait until the fire chief turns his back. He's too close."

Casey's voice was rushed, breathless. "Liz, get me out of here. Now."

"*Hang on*, we've got company."

Judy shouldered the tote and one folding chair. Otis picked up a jockey box. Elizabeth waited until they'd circled the trucks and were beyond the butcher shop. When the coast was clear, she lifted the door handle, but it didn't budge.

Elizabeth pulled harder. Upward was a harder angle. The handle was big enough for one hand, but not quite two. She grabbed the wrist of the hand that gripped the handle and yanked with both. The door wouldn't budge.

"Now, Liz. I'm not kidding."

"It's stuck. Just a sec."

Conversation. Laughter. Brewers, newly free, joked and cheered, lighthearted at the prospect of cleaning up and going home. It had been a Tap Fest they would never forget, but no one was sad to see it end.

Buzz approached. He shook hands with the mayor, their faces solemn. The men looked toward the brewery as they talked. Buzz shook his head. Mayor Roberts pointed toward the beermobile, held both his hands out. Buzz shrugged.

Elizabeth would bet their discussion was one of the future. A future in which she'd have no stake if she didn't get her brother out of Buzz's truck.

"I have an idea." Elizabeth thought of the blinds at school. They opened only after a quick pull downward, then up again. She pulled down.

The door slid downward with a *clang.* This was followed by a *ping, clink.*

"Oh, no. No, no, no."

65

"Liz? Liz! WHAT HAPPENED? Get me out!"

Elizabeth knew, with sickening accuracy, what had happened.

The tricky pin had dropped in place. Casey was stuck.

Her mind raced to remember how Tristan had opened the door. She'd done it earlier, without thinking. Like it was a breeze. Under pressure, hours later, was something else.

A kick. But to the door—or just the handle? Maybe the bumper.

Casey banged on the door. It rattled when he pounded the metal.

"Casey! *Casey.* Stop it. Someone will hear you."

His muffled voice came through the metal door. "Maybe that someone can get me out of this death trap!"

"Panic will only increase the adrenaline to your brain and mine. Give me a minute to think."

"Liz. I am trying to be calm." Casey's voice was stilted. Pressurized. She pictured him pressed to the other side of the door, his cheek to its surface, speaking through the crack in the weather sealant. "But I think I just put my hand in blood, and I am going to freak right out."

"Blood—what? Where?"

His voice whined. "On the corner of the keg freezer. And—maybe on the floor? I'm not going back to verify. Just get me out of here."

Elizabeth puzzled over his news. *Blood inside the beermobile?* She took three steps back, regarded the door.

Tristan had kicked near the lower right side. There'd been the sound of metal popping free and the slide of the door. *Nothing to it.*

Elizabeth considered the surface. Stepped closer to pass her hand across the metal. Spotted her target. Lifted her foot to tap the spot. Practiced her aim.

How hard though?

She scrutinized the door. Inhaled, a deep collection of focus. She released the air, a slow and steady concentration on a duller and dented place in the metal.

"Stand back, Casey," she said.

Elizabeth gritted her teeth, then lifted her foot, knee angled into her chest. Like a pitcher at the mound, she wound up, ready for release.

There was a tap on her shoulder. Elizabeth froze, set her foot back on solid ground, and turned around.

Behind her stood Officer Mackey, Deputy Ryland, and Sheriff Wolf. Not a single official was smiling.

"Would you mind explaining what exactly is happening, Ms. Blau?"

66

"CLINT. UH, SHERIFF. YOU SEE..."

"I'm listening."

The trio waited for her explanation.

"Tristan was trying to *stop* her from stealing. I heard him telling Deirdre he wouldn't help her do it."

Ryland shook his head. "So, because you heard him talking about not stealing, you came out here—why? I'm failing to connect the dots."

Elizabeth met the deputy's eyes. "I had to prove Tristan wasn't the thief. You released everyone which meant Buzz was about to move the beermobile back to the brewery. My proof could be gone."

Wolf had his hands on his hips, his cheeks red with impatience. "Proof—what proof?"

Mackey gave a brief shake of his head. "Tristan had her backpack. He killed her. Took the money."

"There's no motive for murder." Elizabeth crossed her arms over her chest. "Did you even ask him what was in the cans?"

Mackey gave a quick shake of his head. "Excuse me?"

"The cans in Deirdre's backpack. Tristan didn't know they were full of money. Doesn't know."

"Prove it."

Wolf sighed. "Ryland. Mackey. Get Tristan. Officer Fields is sitting with him in his patrol car."

So, Southern is Officer Fields—huh.

When they left, Elizabeth continued. "There's a can inside this beermobile. Firetruck. Whatever it is. It matches the others. I'm willing to bet the only fingerprints on it belong to Deirdre. Furthermore, you'll find Deirdre's prints all over the cans from her backpack—mine, too, on the ones Leia slimed—but you won't find Tristan's."

Wolf was dubious. "Why not?"

Elizabeth unfolded one arm to hold out her hand, palm up. "Simple. He thought they were empty."

Wolf pressed his hand against his mouth, as though to stifle commentary. Rubbed at his chin. After a moment, he asked, "If he didn't kill her, or at least didn't have a motive to kill her, why did he have her backpack?"

"I'm still working that out. But I have a theory. I need to get inside to be sure."

Wolf looked at the ground, rocked forward onto the balls of his feet and then back onto his heels. When he straightened, he met Elizabeth's eyes with his own. "Walk me through this, one more time. From the top. Then I'll decide whether to arrest you for tampering with the scene of a crime."

"You can't do that. I didn't know this was part of the crime scene. Until now, at least. Besides, I told Casey not to touch anything. Especially the blood."

"Blood?" Wolf blinked. "What blood? And where's Casey?"

A voice called out from the other side of the door. "Can someone please let me out of here?"

67

"SHE WANTED SAMPLES?" ENID'S eyes widened, then narrowed again. She set a cup and saucer in front of Elizabeth. "Ah, the recipes. Of course."

Elizabeth nodded. "Ingredient lists are one thing, the final product is another. That way, you can check your success. You need consistency to have a recipe." She sat in a booth at Beans, one of Enid's rainbow, chunky-knit shawls wrapped around her shoulders.

Gary was at the silver espresso machine, steaming milk. "Truth. At its core, a latte is just coffee and milk, but there's an art to that science."

"Exactly," Elizabeth said.

"But why put money in the other cans?"

Enid slid into the chair across from Elizabeth. She twisted backward to respond to Gary. "You know the answer to that. Where better to hide something at a beer festival?"

Gary poured the foamed milk into the mug with a steady hand. "I meant, why did she take the money in the first place?"

"Maybe so she could say she was mugged. Or maybe she needed the cash. Trying to bribe Tristan or someone else."

Enid reached for the plate of cookies she'd set on the table. She selected a peanut butter, then offered the rest to Elizabeth. "All I know is that you blew the pants off that investigation. Don't think I'll be making anything with dry ice for a while to come. How did you know?"

Tristan had popped the tricky door with one solid kick, hands still cuffed. He'd recoiled from the force and almost toppled. Mackey caught him, held him until he was steady while Ryland rolled the door open.

Casey crawled out the moment the door was up. He held one gloved hand out toward the officers, his face pale and clammy, and ran for the nearest trash bin.

Wolf had allowed Elizabeth to remain within earshot as the officers discussed what Casey found. Blood in two places, on the freezer and on the floor.

One lunchbox. One empty, twelve-ounce can, unsealed. Two coolers, open. One pony keg, on its side, tapped. The floor was covered in rivulets of beer. There would be further investigation, detailed analysis. The blood would be identified as Deirdre's.

"It was your ice cream. The sublimation."

Reporters in Billings would announce that Ms. Deirdre Sorenson of Ft. Collins, Colorado had died at a Sheridan County brew fest. She'd slipped, hit her head, and inhaled a lethal amount of carbon dioxide while she lay unconscious. They would state that one Tristan Gibson of Sheridan was charged with a felony for moving the body.

The newscasters wouldn't know Deirdre had been in the process of stealing samples to pass off as her own. That this wasn't the first time.

Elizabeth chose an oatmeal chocolate chip. Gary set a dirty chai, her usual, in front of her before taking the seat opposite with his own caramel macchiato.

"He should have left her there. Buzz would have believed him. Eventually."

"Don't be too sure about that," Enid said.

Future newscasts would report that Tristan pled guilty for a lesser sentence. He'd been out of his mind with grief and fear. Hadn't been thinking straight. Made all the wrong choices.

"So, it wasn't Tristan in the tunnels after all."

Elizabeth shrugged. She wiped the crumbs from her lips with a paper napkin. "Deirdre used them. Or tried to. Buzz didn't seal the tunnel until after she'd left for Colorado. Tristan may have also used them, but he would have known that they didn't lead to the brewery. To him, they would have just been a hiding spot."

Enid took a sip of her tea. She set the oversized, yellow and blue striped mug back on its matching saucer. Hammered, gold circles dangled from her ears. "Sounds like there will be some funding to survey them. Maybe shore a few up. Do some tours like in the big cities."

Elizabeth had been on a dozen tours of the Seattle underground. What secrets would be unearthed beneath the streets of a place like Sheridan?

"Any news from Buzz?"

The brewer had insisted Elizabeth keep the prize money. He said it was only fair since he was in no place to host a keg of her beer.

It had been a few weeks since the contest, but the doors to Maximum Brewing remained shuttered. There'd been a re-call on plastic kegs manufactured with faulty pressure valves. Elizabeth wondered whether Buzz would fix up the building or take the insurance money and run. For now, he'd headed off to Hawaii for an extended vacation.

"Kade's got the beermobile down at his shop," Gary said. "Once they'd collected all the evidence, Buzz wanted it re-painted. Cleaned. A fresh start. Not sure if he's selling it or not."

"Buzz will be alright," Enid said. "He'll know what to do. When the time is right."

"You just want a reason to visit more tropical locations," Gary teased. "Leave me in charge so you can skip across sandy beaches and drink Hemingway daiquiris. Fall in love with some swarthy man while Liz and I are stuck here, land-locked and dateless."

Elizabeth smiled into her cup. "Dateless is better than sad-dled with the wrong man," she said.

"I'll drink to that," Enid said. They clinked mugs together.

"Casey watching Rhett today?"

"Yep. Took him to watch the bike race. With Danny."

Casey had hesitated to ask the brewer on the date. It was a long drive, especially just for the day. But the race was some-what in honor of Danny's ancestor among others. When Eliz-abeth pointed out the macabre name for the hundred-mile event might ring a little insensitive after Deirdre's death, Casey only shrugged. If Danny said no, he said no.

He'd said yes.

Gary snagged a black and white cookie. He took a bite at the split; half chocolate, half vanilla. "How wholesome. Show off his loving uncle vibes."

"Careful. Next thing you know, they'll be each other's plus one for weddings, get matching camping gear, and a dog named Muffin."

"So long as Danny teaches me his brewing secrets, I'll be a model sister-in-law."

Read the Series!

The Sheridan County Mysteries

The Sheriff's Wife(prequel)

The New Teacher(#1)

The Sled Dog(#2)

The Dead Swede(#3)
The Master Mechanic (#4)—Coming Summer 2023

Reviews help readers find books they'll enjoy and authors find people who love their stories.
Please consider leaving a review on your favorite bookshop's website or with Goodreads.

Subscribe to Erin's newsletter to get a free copy of *The Sheriff's Wife*and more at erinlark.com

Afterword

Built in 1923, the real WYO Theater sits at the corner of Brundage and Main in downtown Sheridan. The art deco building was originially named the Lotus and used as a vaudeville theater. I first entered its doors for a Riders in the Sky show, many years ago, and fell in love with the structure and its design. While I have taken liberties with the layout of the building's interior, that should not lessen the draw to visit it or any historic theater. They all benefit from an audience.

I became enamored with the idea of urban tunnels when I stumbled upon the Underground Tour in Seattle. Seattle is only one example of a city that when faced with an architectural challenge made interesting decisions with far-reaching consequences that are worth reading up about (or better yet, visiting to see for yourself). While my cursory search did not reveal a similar scenario in Sheridan, it's rumored there is a tunnel connecting the jail to the courthouse.

Many of us picture beer and cider kegs as large, metal drums. Some breweries use plastic kegs, a choice that became popular when supplies of metal kegs were limited. There are several tragic stories in which plastic kegs exploded with fatal results. Brewers must take care and caution throughout the process.

Acknowledgments

Thank you to my readers for your insight and great energy. I appreciate the time you dedicate to my stories and your engaging feedback!

Three cheers for the work of Terrilani Chong to tighten my prose and her exceptional lessons in diacritics and culture. I wish for everyone to have a pen pal so supportive, even if an ocean away.

Hats off to Paula for tireless editorial attention and to the talented artists at Miblart.

Slàinte Mhaith to all my homebrewer friends and fellow aficionados of a quality beverage, especially my dear friend Don Rogers, master unicycling-juggler Tim "TJ" Carlson, and my brother-in-law Will Brown. You've given me so many mini lessons on brewing and brewing culture—I've learned so much from all of you!

I have the best family whom I love with all my heart.

And as always, a toast to Bryan and Ava, my absolute favorites.

About Erin

From the desert southwest, Erin fell in love with Sheridan County on the banks of Piney Creek. An award-winning science teacher, avid archer, and hack watercolorist, she lives for the outdoors. Erin and her family divide their time between Wyoming, Washington, and Arizona because life is too short to play favorites.

The Dead Swede

Book Three in The Sheridan County Mysteries series

by Erin Lark Maples

Copyright © 2023 by Erin Lark Maples.

Cover designed by MiblArt.

CPSIA information can be obtained
at www.ICGtesting.com
Printed in the USA
BVHW041013210523
664586BV00015B/74

9 781959 116042